About the author

Reginald Marsh-Feiley was born in Monte Carlo. He went to sea at the age of 16 as an apprentice aboard a trampship and graduated as navigating officer to Union-Castle Line passenger liners.

After serving ten years, he left the sea and joined a firm of marine consultants in the city of London.

He now lives with his wife in France and spends half of the year in Aix en Provence and the other half on the island of Ile aux Moines in Brittany.

He paints and has held a number of successful shows in London and France. Still very much attached to the sea he restored a classic Clyde 1909 sloop and sails regularly when in Brittany.

Reginald Marsh-Feiley

A POOR LOOKOUT

A Poor Lookout

ISBN: 978-1-4092-8011-8

Copyright © Reginal Marsh-Feiley 2008

To Petite Fleur, Yvette, Helen, Rob, Aurore and particularly Annaïg without whose help my story may not have been written.

Chapter 1

In Monte Carlo, as was the custom in the late twenties, my father's bank closed for the summer months. He migrated north where he ran a branch of the same bank for the summer season at Le Touquet Paris Plage. It was there that he met and married my mother. At that time, Le Touquet was a fashionable Channel resort for Parisians and British visitors. At the close of the season in September my father would return to Monte-Carlo and resume work there for the winter.

My parents, Robert and Mary Sinclair, lived on the top floor of an apartment overlooking the port of Monaco. I was born at the British Clinic in Monte-Carlo in February 1934.

By this time certain uneasiness was affecting the expatriate population of Monaco due to the rising tide of Nazism in Germany. The social life of Monte-Carlo nevertheless remained unchanged. My father, for his part, having lived and witnessed the horrors of the battle of the Somme in 1916, was of the view that a recurrence of war with Germany was unthinkable and like most residents, hoped that the international situation would have little effect upon the Principality.

The British Royal Navy by then had established Monaco on their itinerary of courtesy calls in the Mediterranean and HMS *Warspite,* a battle-cruiser of the latest design, called at the Principality each year, setting off a number of formal social events, particularly amongst the British colony. Amongst these was a formal party held on board to the music of the Royal Marines' band and for the children, a tea party in the petty officers' mess.

In 1938, I remember being taken on board this huge battleship and being shown its impressive armoury of guns. I can still recall the impeccable cleanliness of the ship with its polished brass and white teak deck, the uniforms, the kindness of the crew and particularly the smell of the warship, which I found subsequently was common to all other large units of the Royal Navy but totally absent from those of the merchant navy. It was during this last visit of the **HMS** *Warspite,* to Monte-Carlo that I knew with absolute certainty, at the age of four, that when I grew up, I would go to sea.

I have a few other vivid memories of Monte-Carlo ; our Italian maid, Antoinette, taught us how to eat spaghetti ; the sun, blue sea, outings to the Botanical Gardens (one winter it was covered in snow), the apartment being decorated for Christmas with branches of orange trees (the oranges used to fall off onto the floor with a bump in the night) our tree all set up with real candles, the Christmas pudding and all things dear to the British tradition which my father maintained religiously. I remember the children's Christmas party given by the British community where I first discovered Father Christmas and in particular, his white beard hanging from elastic on the door of the men's toilet. I also recall being frightened by a black dog which bit my ankle in a restaurant at La Turbie in the hills above Monaco (I have never, since then, been particularly good with dogs) and going fishing and swimming on weekends with my parents. I recall that my sister, Maureen, born eighteen months after me was always much admired whenever we went out. She was very blonde with blue eyes whereas I went unnoticed, being dark and timid. I must admit, even then, to having felt then a certain amount of jealousy!

Life in Monaco was comfortable although I remember little of the day to day household events. My father was somewhat distant with my sister and me and I think that a lot of the time we were looked after by our Italian maid. We spoke a mixture of Italian, English and French, probably in that order although when father was around, we were careful to speak English.

We spent the month of August 1939 in Le Touquet, having travelled there by train via Paris, as was the family custom. This was to be the last time for very many years.

My only distinct memory that holiday was being taken to an air show by my father. Aerobatics performed by daredevil pilots in a series of antique biplanes. One pilot dived down onto the crowd below to pull out just before hitting the spectators but unfortunately, he crashed into the adjacent car-park in an immense ball of fire. Very frightening for a five year old and terminal for the poor pilot.

Because of growing alarm on the international front that year, we left Le Touquet early. Our return journey halfway through August was chaotic if not frantic. The train was packed with people nervously putting as much distance from the northern and eastern borders of France as their situations allowed. I remember that as a precaution, the train was blacked out and the only illumination in our sleeper was a single blue bulb. There were many delays during the run south of Paris. Stopping at Lyon in the middle of the night, the temperature was suffocating. My father got off the train and went in search of something cool to drink. I can still remember the panic when suddenly, the train started to pull out of the station with my father fighting with others to get hold of the carriage door handles to haul himself aboard. He made it just, but lost his bottle of water in the fray.

I think that by then, my parents had begun to realise that war was inevitable. Monte Carlo had no British consul and the nearest with whom we were registered was domiciled at Nice. My father, together with other British residents, called him regularly to try and obtain serious information - the press and local radio at that time were totally unreliable - but the answer, typical of the administration, was to stay calm and do nothing. So, we stayed calm and did nothing. My father went to work as usual but became more anxious as, at last, he started to take note of the fears his Jewish clients, many of whom were German. Stories, which previously, he had thought to be grossly imaginative or exaggerated. Still, we lived in a small independent principality, with its own prince who maintained more or less a neutral front and we reassured ourselves (the British, that is) that we were safe and that no one would dare to harm Monaco. So, the last weeks of August passed with no one quite knowing what to expect, nor what to do.

On the 1st September 1939 the Germans, without provocation and without having declared war, invaded Poland. Bound by treaties with Poland, Britain and France, were forced to declare war on Germans at 5 o'clock on the afternoon of Saturday, the 20 September 1939. I don't remember much of that day except that my parents were glued to the radio trying I imagine, to decipher what was going on. I seem to remember that after the announcement of declaration of war, all the church bells of the principality started to ring as if for a funeral. It was clear, though, that Monaco aligned itself with France and for us there would be so hiding behind a frontier which was nothing more than a state of mind.

So far as we were concerned, however, the months that followed were peaceful and more or less normal. I think that everyone thought that by Christmas, all would be resolved and that an arrangement would be made with Germany to secure peace. In touch with the British consul in Nice, my father was assured that he had no cause to worry.

Fortunately, Italy, who had made sabre-rattling sounds in the direction of Menton, Monaco and Nice, towns which they considered should belong to them, did not in fact declare war on France at that time, but we were not reassured by the fact that sooner or later Mussolini would make his move in our direction.

Christmas 1939 in Monte-Carlo came and went quietly. No festivities to speak of. I was ill over the Christmas period and was unable to join the family for lunch. My parents seemed to spend much of their time listening to the radio but news from the north was released to the public with a great deal of optimism which helped to comfort my father. No Christmas party was held for the British children that year and although life was carrying on more or less normally I think that a cloud of apprehension lay over everything and particularly over Mother who had little faith in the assurances of politicians to the effect that peace would return within the space of a few months. The French were firmly convinced that their line of fortification the line Maginot which comprised invincible forts, could not be taken by the Germans and that consequently the enemy had only to give up any idea of invading France. Unfortunately, this line of protection for what it was worth, extended only to the Belgium frontier. My mother thought that it did not require a military genius to envisage the German army bypassing the Maginot line and simply passing through Belgium to invade France.

So, the months passed and peace being the last thing that Hitler had in mind, the inevitable happened. Germany invaded Belgium, Holland and Luxembourg on the 11th May 1940. There was then no doubt in the minds of the British community in Monte-Carlo of the final outcome although a few still thought that they were safe within the Principality which, like Switzerland, still took extreme pains to advertise its neutrality. With the fall of Belgium and increasing war-like noises from Italy, the British consul in Nice finally manifested himself before the British communities of Monaco and Nice. His instruction from London, he told us, was that all citizens of British nationality should regroup in Cannes for the time being.

A week later, Germany invaded France. Fortunately, we had friends living in Cannes who could put us up and my father arranged for us to leave immediately with a few belongings necessary to subsist for a month or so. My father remained in Monte-Carlo to arrange for the locking up of our apartment and to close down the bank. I think that even then my father believed that within a few months all would be sorted out and then we would return to Monaco. There was one thing however, that must have been on his mind. He had spent much of his life working with Military Intelligence. Not something which was easy to forget, certainly not by the British army anyway, and it was unlikely, in the event of a German invasion, that he be allowed to remain in France or Monte Carlo.

A few days later, we were happily installed in our friend's apartment in Cannes, not far from the Hotel Carlton and the small and very pretty yacht harbour. Things took a turn for the worse however when Italy declared war on France and Britain on the 10th June and the neutrality of Monte-Carlo was finally compromised. This event was followed on the next day midmorning, when, as we were out walking along the sea-front, three or four antique biplanes, presumably flown by young Italian pilots emulating the Wild West flew up and down, low over the sea front, machine gunning all that moved. Mother hauled the two of us into a doorway as bullets hailed down in all directions around us. Fortunately, I don't think that many persons were killed or injured at that time but nevertheless it thoroughly frightened us and gave us our first taste of the war. It did nothing for our peace of mind but at least my father, having closed up shop in Monaco, rejoined us and was in daily contact with the British Consul in Nice.

It was then that we received the awful news that the British government was arranging for the British community in the Cote d'Azur to be repatriated: to where was not made clear. The means by which this was to be affected however was by sea transport; the port of embarkation was to be Cannes. No other details were revealed. Needless to say this caused great consternation and confusion amongst us, none taking kindly to being ordered to leave our homes. Many, like us, had no real attachments in the UK and had nowhere to go. The Consul told us coldly that we had no alternative but to leave; that those who did not, could no longer claim the protection of the British government. We were told to prepare ourselves for immediate embarkation, taking with us only one suitcase of personal belongings per family. Not knowing where we were going, the term repatriation generally led us to believe that this would be the UK, although rumours nevertheless had it that we could just as well end up in Australia, South Africa or Canada. In this unsettled climate my mother packed the bare essentials for us all and we settled down to wait for instructions to embark. Perhaps, were we to embark on a transatlantic liner or a cross-channel ferry, or perhaps a British warship? We had not a clue.

By this time, the German army had reached the outskirts of Paris and the news from the north was not encouraging, to say the least. The British Expeditionary force had been pushed back into the sea at Dunkirk and had been repatriated by a flotilla of small boats, yachts and anything that could float in fact, and which had set out from the south and east coasts of England.

Chapter 2

We waited without news from the Consul, anxious and not knowing what to do or think. Then, on the evening of the 16th June we received news to assemble at six o'clock on the following morning on the quayside of the little port of Cannes.

The morning dawned bright and still, without a cloud in the sky. As instructed, we had a good breakfast and said good-bye to our French friends who were then little more reassured about the future than ourselves. We walked down to the port carrying our one leather suitcase. My mother had dressed with two suits, one over the other and wore her best winter coat with a fur collar. My father had also managed to dress similarly but wore a heavy raincoat. In defiance of orders, dressed in my winter coat, I carried my father's knap-sac on my back in the hope that it would pass unnoticed; not full, but containing articles which might be useful in an emergency, first-aid kit, biscuits and sewing things. We arrived at the port where we were directed onto the quayside by French gendarmes who checked our passports in the company of the British consul. There, we sat down on the ground to await developments.

Much to our consternation, no ship was visible at first sight on the horizon. We numbered about nine hundred men women and children, all bundled together, prevented from moving about or leaving the port by the French police. For the first hour or so the mood of our fellow passengers was reasonably optimistic, although overlaid by anxiety. As the hours passed, the heat became a real problem since we were fully exposed to the sun with little or no shade to be had. My mother, together with a few others commenced complaining to the police asking to be allowed to speak to the British Consul. Their demands were refused. My father was particularly worried in case the lunatic Italian flyers returned to find the entire British population of the Cote d'Azur lined up for target practice. Fortunately, the sky remained free of enemy aircraft; unfortunately so did the horizon remain free of anything that might resemble a ship capable of taking us away from this improvised form of concentration camp. Well before midday, the lack of water and sanitary arrangements had become a major problem. The heat had become unbearable and the health of many persons, particularly the elderly, became a serious preoccupation. My father went in search of water, whether he found any, I can't remember, but I do know that he was very angry when he returned and wanted to forget all about repatriation. He bundled us together and tried to return to the flat in Cannes. He was told by the police on guard that this was not permitted and we had to return to our place on the quayside and wait like all the others.

After having eaten some of our biscuits, there appeared on the horizon a dirty smudge of black smoke which gradually grew and materialised in the form of two cargo ships which anchored off the entrance of the port. They were British ships which had, apparently, just completed discharge of their cargoes of coal at Marseilles. Imagine the reaction of the nine hundred persons waiting in the heat at this apparition. Disbelief, horror and finally anger when it was announced that these were to be our salvation.

Appropriately named the *Ashcrest* and *Salters Gate*, the two vessels were more or less identical. Although not a great deal appears to have been recorded concerning the repatriation of the foreign community of the Cote d'Azur, I have taken this opportunity to set down a little of the information I have managed to obtain.

The "Ashcrest" was built in 1918 and was owned by Crest Shipping of London. She was therefore twenty-two years old on that afternoon in June 1940. Constructed with five cargo holds, she measured some 120 metres long with a beam of 16 metres. Having loaded a full cargo of coal in Cardiff, she sailed in convoy in May 1940 for the port of Caronte, near Marseilles. She arrived there and completed discharged on the 15 June. Instructed to proceed to Cannes, the vessel sailed in the company of the *Salters Gate* which had also discharged coal at Marseilles. The *Ashcrest* was armed with a four-inch gun, probably of the First World War vintage manned by a small contingent of soldiers.

I was later told that our consternation was nothing compared to that of the two captains of the ships who had received orders to proceed urgently to Cannes and had not been informed as to the reason for this diversion. They probably knew however that in any event, they were required to return to join a convoy which was to assemble off the port of Marseilles. I remember little of the confusion and resignation which must have followed orders to embark. We were assigned to the *Ashcrest* together with another 750 hundred hapless souls. The rest of the community embarked on the *Salters Gate*. Amongst those embarked on the *Salters Gate* was the British novelist, Somerset Maughan.

Embarkation of those who appeared to be suffering most commenced to the *Salters Gate*. Having embarked about two hundred persons, she left immediately for Marseilles. It was then our turn to embark little imagining what awaited us. By the time this operation had been completed it was dark. Because of limited deck space, the men were ordered to go down and make themselves comfortable in the holds which were left partially opened, and the women and children were told to remain on deck. We were told by the distraught captain that he regretted the dirty condition of the ship and particularly the holds which still contained considerable heaps of coal dust, but hoped that within a few hours, off Marseilles, we would be probably transferred to a more suitable passenger vessel. He could not offer us any food but told us that his crew would be round to issue us with water to drink. Unfortunately, he said, there would not be sufficient water to allow us to wash. Latrine buckets would be placed at the stern for these who wished to avail themselves of this commodity: please empty over the side when finished. Under dire threats, we were ordered that no lights were to be shown on deck at any time for any reason whatsoever.

Considerably abashed, tiered, dirty and hungry, we sailed from Cannes on a flat calm sea beneath the stars for an unknown final destination but cheered at the thought of being transferred to a passenger ship-visions of showers, food and beds within a few hours. We settled down on deck in the lee of the bridge, my mother sitting on our suitcase for comfort, with my sister and me at each side on her once lovely fur collared coat now coated in grease and coal dust. Father was left to make himself comfortable on the piles of coal and dust remaining in the holds but having survived the battle of the Somme in 1916 and realising that the chances of survival in the hold were slim in the event of the ship being torpedoed, he climbed back up and contrary to orders found himself a little space on deck next to us on which to stretch out.

The night was silent but for the noise of our propeller thrashing the sea astern, for we were riding high in the water.

We saw no other shipping. As dawn was breaking over a flat calm sea, we approached Marseilles roads where a number of cargo ships of various sizes had assembled and were being fussed over by two or three British escort destroyers. One of these detached herself and came over to us and by megaphone swore at us for being late. So late in fact, that the captain was ordered to take his designated place in the convoy that was about to leave without any chance of taking on fresh water or provisions. We understood that the *Salters Gate* had arrived in sufficient time to take on water and food but there was no question, ever, apparently, of her passengers being transferred to another vessel. It was probable that the same applied to the *Ashcrest* and that there never had been any intention of transferring us to another vessel, passenger or otherwise. It seems also that in the general rush the British consular staff at Marseilles were no longer around, presumably having taken the opportunity of finding berths on a vessel rather more salubrious than the poor old *Ashcrest.*

Almost without stopping, we took our place in line with other ships and steamed from Marseilles roads. The convoy was made up of half a dozen ships and a couple of escort destroyers. We were not to see France again for many years.

Chapter 3

Our plight struck us forcibly as, once under way, the captain tried to explain how things stood. In the first place there was little food to go round. For as long as it lasted, we would be given a slice of corned beef together with a piece of bread and a biscuit per person, once a day. A piece of barley-sugar would also be handed out daily to each family. Water, for drinking only, would be distributed three times a day. There being no cups, plates or knives, spoons or forks, we were told to improvise as best we could. As for accommodation, the crew would rig up canvas awnings over the deck as far as they were able to give us some protection from the sun during the day and the heavy humidity during the night. The men would remain in the holds at night. Each family was to make itself as comfortable as possible and try not to move about too much; a few blankets would be given out to the elderly most in need. A line of latrine buckets behind a canvas screen was partitioned into gents and ladies for reasons of propriety. There was no soap and, unfortunately, no other aids to sanitation. Washing was confined to a line-up for the use of a couple of buckets of salt water (coal dust and salt water are incompatible and make slimy paste). My father, for his part, shaved each morning, regardless of having no soap, using a cut-throat and salt water. We had toothpaste and brushes but it took some getting used to using them with salt water and spitting over the side of the ship.

The captain informed us that we were bound for Gibraltar which we should reach in about six days and that unfortunately, there was nothing for it but to be patient. On the subject of security he told us that we were

For the purpose of emergency we were split into two groups and allwell protected by the British Royal Navy destroyers and had nothing to fear. In the event that we were to abandon ship - most improbable he said, there were two small lifeboats, one on each side of the funnel and a few life rafts; these would be reserved strictly for the women and children. How our number should all fit in was not explained. A completed blackout was to be maintained after dark and no smoking was allowed anywhere on board.

Allocated to whatever rafts were available. Lifebelts were given up to families with children although the numbers were totally inadequate.

We were lucky. We shared one lifebelt between the four of us. Fearing that it might be appropriated by some unscrupulous passenger, my mother elected me to be the guardian of this precious item. Consisting of rectangular blocks of cork sewn into a sort of canvas bag fitted with strings, the object smelt musty and, naturally was designed for an adult. I held on to this importantly and trailed it after me wherever I went.

After the second night of sleeping on deck, our personal luck changed largely due my sister Maureen, who although somewhat grubby, was still undeniably a very pretty blonde girl. Whilst the officers and army gun crew were British, the crew was Indian referred to in those days as "lascars". The latter lived aft of the engine-room in cramped and almost inhuman conditions. However, they had one thing going for them, they had their own food which they cooked themselves. Curry and rice! Maureen, who stood out amongst us, being far from timid, seemed to find herself near their galley each day just as lunch was being cooked. It was natural then that a spoonful or two of rice would come her way. Not being nearly as courageous as her, I tagged along timidly behind and was also rewarded with a spoon of rice. I think also, because of her outstanding looks, that my mother together with an elderly Grand Duchess friend was able to persuade one of the junior engineers at a price of a few pieces of jewellery to let us have the use of his cabin. This was little more than a cubby hole but it had a bunk with a blanket and a settee. Maureen and I still slept on the deck but it was incomparable to sleeping outside. Also, super luxury, we had the use of the officer's toilet and toilet-paper. My father still remained in the hold officially but sneaked out to sleep on deck each night. Being drowned in the hold like a rat, (of which, he told us, there were plenty down there), did not appeal to him. In spite of our first class accommodation, meals were taken on deck, a piece of carton as the communal plate and my father's penknife serving as combined knife, fork and spoon. For a cup, my father had managed to scrounge an empty corned-beef tin. This he had cleaned as best he could with sea water but it remained greasy and tainted the water with the flavour of corned-beef.

The enemy, whoever they may have been, left our little convoy strictly alone and we steamed westwards at about nine knots under clear blue skies and flat, calm seas. We had just passed the Balearic Islands, three days after having left Marseilles, when we became aware of the fact that we were gradually dropping astern of the other ships. The convoy slowed to allow us to catch up but by the afternoon of the third day out from Marseilles we were struggling with engine trouble and could no longer keep up with the convoy. One of the escorting destroyers came alongside with the news that they could not wait for us and that we had to do our best to catch up later, once our repairs terminated. She wish us good luck and left quickly to regain the convoy as it disappeared over the horizon.

Our mood therefore could hardly have been described as euphoric as our spirits fell and all our fears returned. We were alone, unprotected and in a war zone. The captain told us not to worry, the repairs would soon be finished and we would be on our way quickly to rejoin the safety of the convoy. Having reassured us, the poor man must have gone down to his little cabin and served himself a very stiff gin and tonic for he must have known then that there was no chance whatsoever of ever catching up with the convoy. We were a sitting duck to whoever might stumble across us and take a shot at us.

At about this time, our fresh water supply ran out. The Chief engineer arranged a system whereby water from the boiler condenser could be piped off. As before, the water ration was minimal, given out three times a day. Insufficient to hoard, we drank our ration as it was, ladled out from a bucket, warm and brackish from the engine-room. In the beginning it took some effort not to bring it straight up again, but we soon got used to drinking warm, corned beef tainted distilled sea water. What remained of the food for the crew, which, till then, had been strictly reserved for the crew, was rationed out amongst us. This did not mean that we had more to eat but its character changed. We now had a sort of watered down soup with bits of corned beef and grains of rice floating about in it if one was lucky. Maureen and me still sneaked into the lascar's galley for our spoonful of rice when no one was looking.

The weather continued to be fine and at midday, the sun beat down on us mercilessly. It reflected off the calm water adding to our discomfort making it impossible to find a cool place. Being stopped in the water, we lost our breeze caused by the forward motion of the ship and lay there sweating and suffocating, waiting for the sun to sink below the horizon. In addition, we were tormented by flies. Where on earth these had come from we couldn't guess, but our own personal conditions of hygiene hardly helped.

Chapter 4

On the morning of the 22 June in a position 25 miles south of Alicante, the captain announced that temporary repairs had been completed and that we were to resume our course for Gibraltar at a reduced speed. This announcement was greeted with loud cheers and clapping. By this time the condition of the passengers had deteriorated. Medical assistance was confined to basic medicines from the ship's medical chest administered by the captain and a doctor one of our group passengers. Underway at last, we were once again able to benefit from a slight breeze. What, perhaps, was not so good was the fact that on stoking the main engine boilers to get up a head of steam, thick black smoke emerged from our tall, thin funnel, thus announcing our presence to any and every vessel, friendly or not, which may have been cruising, hull down, below the horizon. I imagine that this great pall of black smoke trailing aft must have done nothing to boost the captain's morale and sense of security. Had we tried to do this on purpose, we could not have done better.

Whether it was this or not, I shall never know, but as we made our painful way westwards trailing our smoke behind us, we were shaken out of our mid-afternoon stupor that day by the frightful clanging of the alarm bells. Someone shouted "a submarine"! There was a massive surge of people falling over themselves to get to the port side for a look. There, abeam, at a distance of about 1000 metres was a mass of white turbulence in the water out of which the grey form of a submarine emerged and turned towards us. The alarm bells and ship's whistle sounded causing a minor panic amongst the mass of people on deck pressing to get near to the lifeboats. My mother took advantage of the confusion to wrap me up in our treasured lifebelt. Poor Maureen, no lifebelt. She still hasn't forgotten this!

What we must have looked like to the submarine commander, I have no idea but we must have resembled a sort of derelict garden shed with our bits of tarpaulin flapping about over the decks. Whatever, the submarine commander obviously took an instant dislike to us and decided to sink us to put us out of our misery. He fired two torpedoes almost simultaneously and was confident presumably of the holocaust this would provide, when suddenly, our little four inch gun unexpectedly opened up in defiance and fired back at him with short sharp bangs which half frightened us to death. The two torpedoes ran fast straight and true and converged directly at mid point aft of the bridge, just where we were standing, to pass beneath our keel without, I suspect, more than a few centimetres to spare. I can still remember vividly the two tracks left by the torpedoes and the stillness of those around us, petrified awaiting the big bang.

Having missed us, the submarine then opened fire with her deck gun. Three rounds were fired but again, fortunately, they missed. By this time our gunners had got themselves organised and had opened fire in reply to the submarine's second shot. It seems that our riposte to frighten away the submarine for it submerged and disappeared from site. In any event, we stayed awake on deck all night afraid of being attacked again. However the night passed without further incident.

The following day dawned fine and calm with the horizon clear of any signs of shipping. The captain told us that the submarine which had attacked us had not been a German

U-boat, but had been an Italian, possibly on his way back to base in Italy. He informed us also that as a result of the attack he had radioed to the Spanish authorities for permission to enter their territorial waters. Because of the nature of his "cargo" this had been given, somewhat reluctantly, we were given to understand. The days passed slowly with a short, rapid stop one night to allow the burial at sea of a woman who had succumbed during the day.

Seven days after having left Cannes, we steamed around Europa Point and berthed in Gibraltar. That afternoon, 255 refugees were disembarked from the *Ashcrest* under the supervision of the naval authorities. We were amongst this group. The *Ashcrest* duly sailed in convoy from Gibraltar on the 28 of June with 11 other vessels including the *Salters Gate*. She arrived in Liverpool with her remaining 495 evacuees on the 8 July 1940.

As a tribute to those of the British merchant navy who lost their lives during the war, I should like to add that about four months later the *Ashcrest* loaded a cargo steel at Sydney, Nova Scotia for discharge at Liverpool. On the 7 December, she became detached from her convoy due to damage to her steering gear. Drifting helplessly in a position north of the west coast of Scotland, she was torpedoed on the night of the following day by the submarine U-140. The *Ashcrest* sank with the loss of all 37 members of her crew.

Chapter 5

My recollection of our arrival in Gibraltar is very hazy since by then I was sick and very weak. I remember being carried down the gangway in the arms of a nurse and waking up in the hospital of the British troopship *Dunera* in the presence of my mother and a doctor. Maureen, I think, had fared much better than me and had not been hospitalised. I was told that we had sailed from Gibraltar but no one was able to say where we were going. Since, at that time, we were heading westwards, it was rumoured that we were heading for the USA or perhaps Canada.

Within two or three days I was able to move about and leave the hospital deck. I was able to visit my father who had been confined to the lower decks in the company of men of our *Ashcrest* compatriots billeted with the troops. They had each been given a hammock, mess tin and cutlery and told to have their meals in the soldiers' mess. Although many of the men of our group were of elderly aristocratic lineage and had served as officers during the Great War, their pleas for recognition as such and privileged treatment were ignored. My father on the other hand had a certain sense of humour about this and quite happily accepted his lower-deck condition.

Our days were rigidly controlled and commenced with boat drill at about six o clock in the morning. All hands on deck and mustered at their respective boat stations, women and children included. Thereafter the day was punctuated by alarms followed by further boat drills. I have little recollection of those days other than for two very precise memories. The first was that I made re-acquaintance with fruit jelly, green, yellow, red and orange which I had first sampled on the *Warspite*. I can't say that I looked forward to these treats but the shapes and colours were beautiful. The second was the formation of other ships around us, seemingly unmoving, as we steamed through calm seas and sunny skies. There seemed to me to be hundreds of ships close around us, the pattern changing only when an escorting destroyer zigzagged amongst those ships which were having difficulty in holding their station or speed. Night times were bad, standing-to at boat stations when a ship amongst us was torpedoed. On the following morning her place would be taken by another and ranks closed up.

Our course seemed to change each two or three days and by the time the first week had passed, we had no notion of where we were or indeed, where we were going. We must have been heading in a northerly direction for the weather gradually changed, becoming cold and grey. The sea, although no longer calm, was moderate but not really rough and this did nothing for many of our group who took to their hammocks and bunks. They were incapable of participating in the boat drills. Nevertheless it was surprising to see how efficient the military police was in persuading us to climb up on deck in the rain and cold wind. Some had the feeling that perhaps a speedy torpedo might be a good way out of their misery.

We were joined by another convoy somewhere in the North Atlantic and this great armada of ships steamed north-westerly; still not a word of where we were bound. Although conditions for us were incomparable to those of the *Ashcrest* the morale of our group deteriorated. More and more ships were torpedoed, disappearing each night and the escort activity became more and more sustained as though they were sheep dogs whose charges, under attack from a pack of wolves, were trying to run away.

One morning at daybreak we found ourselves alone but for a few ships and escorts, the bulk of the convoy having steamed off toward another destination. It was announced that we had entered the Irish Sea by the north and were expected to arrive shortly at Liverpool where we were to disembark.

Although still summer, it was cold, wet and windy when we docked there in the early afternoon. We, of the *Ashcrest* with our small bundles of belongings, were herded down a wet and slippery gangway into a gloomy immigration and customs hall.

Chapter 6

Assembled in the draughty hall, we were told that the country was being bombed heavily by the Germans and it was thought that the possibility of them using poison gas was not to be ignored. In view of this therefore, HM Government had arranged to issue, free to each one of us, a gas mask, basic utility type. We were lined up and each given a square cardboard box to which was attached a string so that it could be carried across the shoulders. We were told that our gas masks were to be carried at all times wherever we went. The masks themselves, although fitted with apparently adjustable head straps, were ill fitting and hideous looking. They were made of black rubber which smelt horribly. The eyepiece was oval and made of some sort of embryo perspex. When instructed to put it on, two things happened. First, I could not breathe and second, the eyepiece steamed up and I could not see. I can't remember how the others felt about their first contact with these things but I suspect that in the event of us being attacked with gas we would go for the wet handkerchief over mouth and nose option, rather than die suffocated in a sort of Mickey Mouse mask. Fortunately the efficiency of the masks was never to be put to the test. Later however, at school, when regular gas-mask drill was obligatory, I grew to hate these things (Many years later, when I was to find myself trapped in the hold of a ship on fire, I was to remember the same feeling of claustrophobia, wearing the mask of a modern breathing apparatus).

We were then given tin mugs of hot sweet tea and told to wait, still without having been informed about what the authorities had in mind for us. I think that it was very likely that once embarked aboard the *Dunera*, we had been forgotten and it came as a surprise to those in Liverpool to find a couple of hundred refugees with nowhere to go to. After some hours, a passenger train was shunted alongside the immigration and customs hall and we were told that we were being taken to London where accommodation would be found for us.

I don't know why, but I think we all expected to be housed in hotels of the type we had known in Monte-Carlo and the French Riviera. On arrival at Euston station in London, we were rounded up and put aboard some old busses and taken to the YMCA Hostel at Finsbury Park, a centre for young men cleared for the occasion. We were each given one army blanket and a pillow, told to bed down in the dormitories, men in one and women and children in another. Basic food was available in the refectory. The atmosphere was far from friendly and we were treated with little more than veiled contempt.

We were given three days to find our own lodgement after which time the YMCA would be closed to us since apparently it was designated to accept several hundred Polish refugees. During the couple of days that followed my father was able to visit the head office of his bank in Lombard Street and was given a temporary job in a branch office in Edgware road.

Tramping the streets for hours, he was able to find a room in a terraced house in Finsbury Park, not far from the park itself. Thus commenced our life in the UK. We were home, safe and sound! It's strange to think that the experience aboard the *Ashcrest* combined with that of the *Dunera* did not shake me from my determination to go to sea when I grew up.

Finsbury Park had the advantage of being somewhere where we could walk and play during the day. It was also fascinating for me since it held a unit of antiaircraft guns and, best of all, a huge barrage-balloon. An enormous silver painted sausage with fins which floated high in the sky, tethered on the ground by means of a steel wire wound onto the drum of a winch. The soldiers manning this were kind to us and very friendly.

There were hundreds of these balloons floating high in the sky over London at that time. The idea behind this was to form an aerial barrage to prevent enemy aircraft from approaching targets of strategic importance such as London Docks and mainline railway stations. The down side of living in Finsbury Park was that at night it became the target for the German air force. Since we were close to Euston Station it was not surprising that each night it rained down on us all manner of high explosive and incendiary bombs, land mines and anti-personal mines (which looked a bit like toys), called butterfly bombs but which, when handled, blew one's head off.

The weather during those few months spent at Finsbury Park was fine and warm. The nights were fine and clear, without clouds to obscure the German air force bombers from observing their targets in detail. The blackout imposed upon us below was almost superfluous and the bombers were able to locate Euston station and by the same token, Finsbury Park without any trouble at all.

The air-raid sirens would sound at around nine o'clock each night and the local population would head off for an assortment of air-raid shelters. The most popular of these were the Underground stations whose platforms had been equipped with tiers of wooden bunks. Those who took to this form of shelter soon become adepts and took up their places as soon as the last train had passed, an hour or so before the sirens sounded. They had their bunks and woe betide anyone who tried to usurp their places. The stations were so popular that when all the bunks became occupied, the people simply lay down along the platforms in rows. It was not unknown for shouts and screams to be heard in the middle of the night due to the rats and mice that occupied the tunnels which came foraging amongst the sandwidges and the tightly packed bodies of the new occupants. Much less popular were the shelters provided in parks, public places and street corners; for example, one of the shelters in London Zoo was located ironically in the Monkey House and received a direct hit. Even less safe were the so-called Andersen Shelters which the population were urged to build in their gardens and which comprised a hole dug in the ground covered with curved sheets of corrugated iron over which one placed the earth that one had excavated from the lawn. These had a tendency to flood each time it rained and many were to drown in their own shelters, the results of stupid accidents.

Chapter 7

Even with all hell being let loose above our heads, no amount of official pressure would persuade my parents to join the crowds in search of underground shelter. They decided that to die in our beds was preferable to being crushed or buried alive, the fate of so many poor people who died in a so called bombproof shelters.

It was now the beginning of September 1940. Each night, after the air-raid siren had given the alarm, we would lie in our beds listening for the first squadrons of German bombers as they approached London. They came in waves, a droning sound which rose and fell; a sound full of menace and which, as the days passed began to upset me more and more. The bombs rained down, making a whistling sound as they fell and exploded all around us. The noise of the explosions was not, in itself, so frightening since it was generally muffled by the houses themselves as the blast blew them down into a great heap of rubble. On occasions the sound resembled a pile of bricks being tipped out the back of a lorry. Added to the noise of the anti-aircraft guns was the sound of the ambulances fighting their way through the littered streets to pick up the injured and dead intelligible cries of the air raid wardens and helpers.

On the principle that all that goes up must come down, the nightly chaos was added to by a rain of red hot shrapnel, the remains of exploded anti aircraft shells which sliced down into the streets and through the roofs and attics of houses below. Listening to all this on a regular nightly basis was, to me, a living nightmare. I did not understand why anyone should want to kill us and in my confused mind I used to offer up a sort of prayer to the German pilots, asking them to leave us alone. Maureen, my little sister, usually slept through all this although how she managed this, I still have no idea. My parents maintained a stiff upper lip and waited for the raids to finish as though, by ignoring it, it would all go away. We were lucky, half the houses on the streets around us were reduced to heaps of rubble, but ours still stood, scarred and battered, but whole.

Our living conditions in Finsbury were of the poorest and it was clear that we couldn't remain there much longer. My mother had, by the end of September managed to trace and contact part of her family who had emigrated to London during the French Revolution in 1792. Still living in London were four spinsters, far removed cousins, whose ages ranged from eighty to ninety years old. The eldest, Cecile, was in a Carmelite convent, a closed and contemplative order almost impossible to speak to, whilst the other three sisters lived together in Kensington. Although they lived in a large house bordering a square, they had no means of housing us themselves but set about searching for accommodation for us. They eventually found something, reasonably close to them, in Elgin Crescent. A mid-nineteenth century town house, three floors, basement and pillared entrance, typical of that area. The house was divided into flats and was occupied by a number of families but the basement, below street level but opening out into a small courtyard down a few steps from the street, was vacant. It was furnished in cast-off Victorian furniture which had seen better days and was dreary and dingy with barely enough light. Unfortunately, it also smelt bad, cats and cabbage, but it was infinitely better than Finsbury. However, like Finsbury Park, it was not too far removed from another mainline railway station, Paddington which again was a favourite target for bombs of all descriptions. At night almost all the population retired to various underground stations. Not far was Notting Hill Gate and being the deepest, featured a full house each night.

The air-raids were, if anything, worse than before and at night it seemed as thought the whole of central London was ablaze. To give an idea of the destruction caused by bombs between September 1940 and May 1941, about one and a half million people were made homeless and about fourteen thousand were killed.

My father by this time, had managed to find employment with a bank in Regent Street. It was by way of a number of his clients that he made contact with and became involved with the Free French movement in London.

By this time, my fear of air-raids had increased and my health was again, not brilliant. I lay in our bed at night (shared with Maureen) and shook and trembled until the All Clear was given during the early hours of the morning. Another preoccupation that worried me was that I had been told that I would have to go to school. This did not appeal to me, having had absolutely no contact whatsoever previously with children of my own age. The problem for my parents was that all the schools in central London had been closed and the children evacuated to towns and villages in the country, far away from London.

It was clear that we could not continue to live in Kensington and that it was only a matter of time before the house we were living in was transformed into a heap of smouldering rubble (in fact, it somehow managed to survive). In any event we were not given any choice. The local authorities had decided that all the children were to be evacuated from London. It was allowed, exceptionally, that our mother could accompany us. We were told that we would be accommodated in the cottage of a family of farm labourers, part of an agricultural college in the small village of Long Sutton in Hampshire. My father, of course, was to remain in London.

Chapter 8

By then it was early spring of 1941. It was then that my personal problems were to overtake me. Being seven years old, and not having been to school before, I was two years behind other children. I was immediately enrolled in the village primary school and overnight confronted with serious difficulties. Firstly, I couldn't understand the strong rural Hampshire accent so that when the teacher spoke to me, I had no clear idea of what was required of me. I just stood, when finally persuaded to sit down at a desk and told to write my name on a slate with a piece of chalk, I did so with some difficulty. The slate was not big enough to accommodate all my name. Worse was to come. My hand received a nasty blow from the teacher's ruler. The piece of chalk was torn out of my left hand and placed in my right hand and I understood that I was to start again, using my right hand. I had never written with my right and was quite incapable of doing so. Thus started my school career. The other boys jeered at me and I was sent to the corner where I sat on a stool facing the wall. I didn't cry but my thoughts were filled with violence. I fancied that it might be a good idea if some German bombers could make a small diversion one night in the direction of Long Sutton and reduce the school to a heap of rubble.

Three other factors were not to better my lot amongst them, or the teacher, for that matter. The first was that it had been noted that I was a Roman Catholic. The common belief amongst the boys was that only vagrants, Irish labourers, Jews and criminals were Roman Catholics. The second was that I was dressed differently - shoes, instead of hobnailed boots, no flat-hat and worst of all, short socks. It was quite clear that I was a sissy. The third was that I was a foreigner and that the lot of a foreigner at the beginning of the war, was to be beaten up regularly. The first days at school always seemed to end with my being put in the corner, face to the wall. For the return home from school, I ran the gauntlet of boys lying in wait or chasing me to beat me up or to try and get my trousers off, (a favourite past-time in boys' schools in those days).

I must have worked it out that if I dressed like the other boys and spoke like them, I might survive. My mother was not easy to persuade. She finally bought me a pair of hobnailed boots and some jumble sale clothes; no flat-hat, though. I began to acquire a good strong Hampshire accent. I could do nothing about my writing except to be regularly beaten over the left hand by the teacher's ruler. Nor could I change my religion, but it was a good start. Although overpowered by boys bent on my destruction, I gave as good as I got, particularly when it came to kicking with my new hobnailed boots. I can remember taking long devious routes to reach home in the afternoons and becoming quite adept at sneaking past the ambushes that were set for me.

My mother's protestations at school concerning my education were met with indifference. After all, she was a foreigner. Looking back, I think that her isolation at Long Sutton was not very dissimilar to mine but without the physical abuse, of course. Our previous way of life was really too remote from rural village life. Nevertheless it had two big advantages. Firstly we were not likely to be killed by bombs and secondly, we fared reasonably well with regard to food - something which had not been readily available in London. Rook pie, for example, was a favourite, something of a local delicacy once the lead shot had been spat out.

The months passed and gradually I adapted to school life. Another incident however, was to leave its mark. The school was visited one day by a dentist in a sort of caravan. I was forcibly dragged into this and my teeth were examined. It seemed that what the dentist saw offended him since he decided to pull out a couple of my back teeth. I had no idea what this involved, but was soon to find out. He started by half filling my mouth with cotton-wool. Needless to say, I gagged, which displeased our dentist. The next stage was to spray the cotton-wool with ether or chloroform whose sickly smell nearly made me pass out. By this time I was reduced to jelly, wishing I was back under the bombs. The two offending teeth were wrenched out with a pair of pliers after which the chloroform soaked cotton-wool was removed and I was given a glass of water and sent packing, spitting blood and feeling sick. My mother was horrified and complained to the school that there had been nothing wrong with my teeth. Total indifference from the teacher, needless to say. From then on my visits to a dentist were to be overshadowed by trauma which lasted many years into my life.

My father visited us irregularly at weekends and told us of the continuing nightly air-raids. By this time the Germans were concentrating on destroying the docks at London. Some nights, out in the country, we were able to see the loom in the sky of London burning. During these visits, my father became more and more concerned about the effects of my local education. My manners were rough, affected to be like the others, and I spoke in a pronounced rustic Hampshire accent.

Chapter 9

We had been in Long Sutton for about a year when my father decided that it was time to remove us from this environment. He had met a client of the bank who had told him that she possessed a house in Friern Barnet, in North London, which she was willing to let to us. North London was relatively free of bombing and the risks were incomparable to those of central London. We moved there in the spring of 1942 and installed ourselves in a comfortable suburban house with a front and back garden. It was fully furnished, modern, and was even equipped with a washing-machine, the first that I had ever seen. School was sought for us both since my sister Maureen by now had reached school age. This took the form of an upmarket private school some fifteen minutes walk from the house. I think that my parents, were reasonably happy in the knowledge that our immediate future would be more or less adapted to the sort of life we had led in Monte-Carlo.

For me however, the new school turned out to be another cultural shock. Here I was then, the rustic Hampshire lad, sat in amongst very middle-class suburban children. I still had my hobnailed boots and country jumble sale clothes. It was accepted that I could use my left hand to write, but my level of writing and arithmetic was a year or more behind that of children of my own age. My appearance was changed rapidly to conform to the appropriate standing. I was outfitted with the school uniform complete with tie, blazer, pullover and cap. I nevertheless could do nothing for the moment about my rustic manner of speech. But this was to change gradually in the months that passed. Maureen had started in the same school and each day, we went off together in our new school uniforms. She was much quicker to adapt than me and quickly made friend whereas I didn't.

The air-raids still continued and although there was existed an anti aircraft battery at the corner of our road which made an infernal din when it opened up, I had more or less lost my fear of being killed each night. The in-thing was to collect shrapnel lying in the road on the way to school. One night the house one of our neighbours received a direct hit and was demolished. The occupants were killed and I remember that against one of the walls that was still standing, the bath hung there in space.

One afternoon during the Easter holidays of 1942 mother treated us. She took Maureen and me to see the new Walt Disney film Bambi which had just reached us from Hollywood. The cinema was in Leicester Square and for us, our visit to the West End was very exciting. The film was half way through when it stopped and the cinema manager climbed up on the stage in front of the screen and announced that a very heavy air-raid was taking place outside. He suggested that the audience should seek refuge in the shelter which was beneath the cinema. Nobody moved, the audience considered that to die watching Bambi was preferable to being buried alive in a dark cellar underground. The manager, faced with this mini revolt of his audience, applauded our decision and told us that the show would go on. I saw the film accompanied by violent explosions, tremors and the scream of bombs falling on the buildings around us.

We saw Bambi and survived.

This sadly was not the case for many around us for when we left the cinema, Leicester Square had been partially demolished and was on fire. We hurried to the underground station, almost blocked with people sheltering, through the rubble, the broken glass and the smoke. We returned home for tea having abandoned the idea having it at Lyons Corner House in the Strand! This small incident shows to what extent the people of London were prepared to go to get away from the daily horrors of death and destruction.

The government exhorted us to Dig For Victory. This meant that it was our patriotic duty to dig up rose beds and lawns and plant potatoes and cabbages. Around us there didn't appear to be a great following. People still grew their flowers and cut their lawns, much preferring to die, if necessary, in an English country garden than in a cabbage patch. My father, perhaps for the first time in his life, found himself with a garden, rose beds, trimmed hedges and lawn. Everything, in fact, that a suburban house worthy of the name could wish for. He decided that in terms of economy and patriotism that it would be a good idea to follow the exhortations of the government. He commenced to dig up the roses and flowers and plant cabbages and potatoes. He dug up the front lawn and planted carrots and turnips. Added to this, he hammered up some old packing cases and converted them into cold-frames and rabbit hutches.

My parents followed the progress of the war on the radio. News was bad on all fronts. The German submarines were decimating our convoys and there was a shortage of basic food at home. The radio news bulletins were heavily censored with the result that the news that we were fed probably bore little relation to the truth. My mother seemed to support all this with fortitude but on the 27th November 1942 she heard over the radio that the French fleet had been scuttled at Toulon; battle ships, cruisers, an air craft-carrier and others, in all 135 warships. It was first time that I saw my mother crying.

Chapter 10

The winter of 1942 was exceptionally cold. It was during this period that my father's, closest friend, Richardson, turned up at the house with his son, Michael, who was on leave. Michael was everything I wanted to be. He had been educated at the Royal Naval College at Dartmouth since the age of twelve and was then a midshipman serving aboard a destroyer on escort duty in the Arctic Ocean protecting supply convoys to Archangel in Russia. A murderous life which he had so far survived. His accounts of life at sea fired my imagination which renewed my ambition to go to sea. Nothing else counted. In any event, I hated gardening and planting turnips. I hated school as well but Michael told me that if I wanted to go to sea, I would have to be good at arithmetic and geography.

Every now and then my father brought home men who stayed with us for two or three days. During the next three years some of them made several visits to our home whilst others never returned. I was old enough to know now that these men formed part of the French resistance underground movement. I can't remember them all but two in particular stood out. I mention them because both of them left a deep impression on me. I must say that when they were at our house, they made a great fuss of Maureen and me, particularly a young French air force officer (at least, he was dressed as such). He was later to be captured by the Gestapo and tortured. He took his own life by tearing out his throat with a nail rather than reveal the names of his colleagues. The other was known to us as Renaud. He was older but over dinner at home, he told marvellous stories and made us laugh when, perhaps, there was not much to laugh about. He stayed with us many times He was quite fearless, except that jumping out of an aeroplane with a parachute at night over occupied France really terrified him.

He was eventually denounced to the Gestapo and was shot down and killed in a street in Paris.

By September of 1943 arrangements had been made for Maureen and me to be removed from our school in Friern Barnet - constant aggravation with the headmistress - and placed in a convent, a girls private school in North Finchley. The year that followed was to be the most cheerful schooldays of my life.

The convent was run by Dominican nuns for about 300 girls. Amongst all these girls were two boys only. I never learnt how it was that the two were there, particularly since one was Jewish and the other Protestant. Although we were treated as equals with the girls so far as schooling was concerned, we were nevertheless spoilt by the nuns. The slice of home made cake, for example, sold to the girls at the morning break for one penny, was generously given to us free of charge if we accepted the end slices which were slightly overcooked. They were also slightly thinner than the regular slices. Still, it was a kind gesture and obviously one that I have never forgotten. Whenever I see a slice of Madeira cake, I am reminded of a small nine year old boy queuing up with hundreds of girls, and not one of them wanting to beat me up. There was, of course, one girl in particular. She was called Margaret. She had curly red hair and we used to have wrestling matches on the playing field. She nearly always won. She used methods which were hardly fair and which I couldn't really apply to her, but she was so lovely and sat next to me in class.

At the school Christmas concert that year, I was included in the choir. It was then that I discovered that I would not sing at any price. Some sort of psychological hang-up or whatever. I have never been able to sort that one out and am still unwilling to sing.

The bombings, by the end of the year 1943, had largely petered out over London and other than for sporadic daytime raids it was reasonably quiet. I can remember my parents celebrating the Allied landings on the Normandy beaches on the 6th June 1944. We were all huddled around the radio that night, listening to the news.

In retaliation, the Germans resorted to a new secret weapon, the V.1. bomb. The first of these hit London a week after the landings. They were particularly inhuman and antisocial. Jet propelled, they flew on their own, making a noise not unlike a badly tuned motorbike. They could be heard coming miles away, five or six at a time. One after the other, their engines would cut out and they would then glide down silently into whatever lay in their path. The amount of explosive they carried was sufficient to take out half a street of houses at a time. The antisocial side was that one prayed, as they headed towards you that their engines would keep running until they had passed overhead. In other words, pray that it would fall on the heads of others a little further up the road! Fortunately, this type of bombing did not last long. The launching pads in northern France was the object of frequent attacks by our own bombers and were also vulnerable to sabotage by the French Resistance.

The V.1 flying bombs were replaced by the V.2. This was the first of the modern rockets. Launched from strategic points in Europe, they dropped down onto London silently and blew out whole streets at a time. We lived with these with a certain fatality; one was simply blown up or one weren't. Fortunately they also didn't last long, a few months at the most, and after that we were left alone to ponder upon the destruction that our own air forces, American and British, were raining down on the German cities. Each evening, I would watch from my bedroom window as wave after wave of heavy bombers heading south passed overhead in close formation.

Chapter 11

The war in Europe ended with the unconditional surrender of the Germans on the 8th May 1945. A few weeks before that, I was just 11 years old, my mother took me to Gaumont cinema in North Finchley. I mention this because of the deep impression it made on me. We did not see Walt Disney's Bambi this time. We saw, instead the British troops entering the extermination camp of Belsen, a small village some fifty miles south of Hamburg in Germany. My mother had insisted that, as a representative of the next generation, I should see and remember the awful scenes that were shown and never forget to tell what I saw to my own children.

For us, the children, the war ended with a tea-party. The residents of many of the streets locally had set out trestle tables in the road to which all the children were invited to eat as much home made bread, jam and cakes as they could. There were even jellies, saved from before the war presumably set aside with great optimism for the occasion. No sell-by by dates then! The grownups, well, they celebrated later, dancing in the street.

Very quickly, in the weeks that followed, something changed. People no longer went out of their way to help others as they had during the war. There was even less in the shops and rationing was re-enforced with new cuts.

For us, the end of the war presented another major problem. The people to whom the house in Friern Barnet belonged wanted to return to London and asked us to leave. Searching for accommodation in the weeks that followed the end of the war was a heartbreaking affair. Everywhere from the countryside, families were returning to London. Many of their homes had been destroyed and the housing shortage was acute. Nothing was being done seriously about clearing the bombs sites and starting the rebuilding, probably because of the lack of building materials.

Finally, in July, my father found a couple of rooms in the attic of an Edwardian house in Muswell Hill not far from where we had lived throughout the greater part of the war. The house smelt of old cabbage and cats. The rooms were sublet to us by an old witch of a woman who imposed all sorts of restrictions. The antique bathroom complete with gas water-heater that leaked and meter into which one had to feed shillings, was located two floors down. A miserable cubby hole, with a stone sink and a cold water tap, served as a kitchen although there was no cooker or gas-ring. This was located on a landing between our rooms and the bath. My parents occupied one room and the other was where Maureen and I slept on a vinyl covered convertible settee. This was where we lived and had our meals. It was a miserable, dark and wretched place. Furthermore there were holes in the ceiling where shrapnel had broken through the roof tiles and we could look up from our bed at night and see the stars. Heating, if one could call it that, was supplied by a single-bar gas fire which consumed shillings at an astronomical rate. There was talk amongst the parents that we would soon all be returning to Monte-Carlo and that our present situation was merely temporary.

Arrangements had been made for me to go to a private school for boys. This was a very long bus ride from Muswell Hill; Maureen stayed at the convent. In started my studies with enthusiasm but this soon wore off as I discovered that teaching was a matter of beating information into a pupil's skull, very often with the use of a ruler or cane. In addition to this, the discipline imposed upon us was Dickensian. No speaking at meals, or in class for that matter, unless one was addressed by the master, and minor infringements severely dealt with on the spot. Serious crimes were handled by the head master who used a sort of boot sole attached to a wooden handle to beat the hell but of one's bum. I sampled this a couple of times; sitting down afterwards was a bit of a problem. Another example of the sort of discipline enforced. A boy complained that his fountain-pen had been stolen. The whole school, all six hundred boys, was made to line up on the playground. The boy responsible for this theft was asked to own up. Nothing happened; no boy came forward and owned up. We stood there for an hour. It started to rain and we were soon soaked through and shivering; still nothing happened. Finally, a quarter of an hour later, a white-faced boy in a state of near collapse stumbled forward and admitted having taken the pen. We never saw the boy again, nor did we ever see the object of the theft - the victim proudly displayed a new fountain-pen some days later - and I wonder to this day if, in fact, the boy who admitted to the theft had been the true culprit. He didn't look like a criminal to me, more like a victim.

Unfortunately I was not a brilliant scholar. It took a substantial number of cuffs around the ears to instil the basics of elementary algebra in my head. The maths master was quite violent and beside himself at times. Latin, compulsory of course, was also a tricky subject. Who needed Latin at sea? I was not much good at sport either. Getting my already beaten up ears rubbed off in a rugby scrum left me indifferent. Cricket was all right but I was never to be a leading top scorer. Can do better, said my school reports. Still, I managed and coped with the school's system of rough judgement and instant retribution reasonably well. It must be said that discipline in the home was tight also, although not expressed in terms of corporal violence as we say nowadays. I don't think that we had a lot to laugh about in Muswell Hill.

The war having finished, my parents set about seeing what could be done about our belongings in Monte Carlo which had been abandoned in 1940. I think that having written for months during the early part of 1946 and getting no answers from the British Consul in Nice, nor from the Monegasque authorities in Monaco, my father decided that the only thing to do was to return there himself to see what had happened and possibly to see if there was any chance of taking up life there where we had left off.

In the summer of 1946 therefore, we all left for Monte Carlo by train, crossing the Channel at Dover and changing trains in Paris. My recollections of what happened then, for some reason, are very vague. I remember that we looked at several properties with a view to buying or renting. Our flat had been requisitioned and was now occupied by strangers and most of our possessions had disappeared. My father's bank was still closed down and no one could say if and when it might reopen. Things had changed and all our friends were gone.

This was a crushing blow for my parents from which, I think, they never fully recovered. Discouraged and disappointed we all returned to Muswell Hill to try and fashion a new life in England. My father was never to return to Monte Carlo although subsequently my mother went back to France regularly for holidays where she stayed in Nice.

A few belongings which were found in some abandoned store were duly crated up and shipped to us in Muswell Hill.

Needless to say all the items of value had disappeared but there remained a few silver spoons and forks which had been mixed up with kitchen cutlery together with some 18th century crystal glasses which had been overlooked. My father's valuable stamp collection had also not been discovered, hidden amongst books, old papers and periodicals. All this some months later, arrived at Muswell Hill, damp and covered with mould, (it took my father several years to clean up his collection of stamps) and was piled up in my parent's room and into whatever space was left in the living room.

Chapter 12

Having taken the decision not to return to Monte Carlo, my parents set about trying to find somewhere to settle down. Perhaps my father's efforts at Digging for Victory had left in him a desire to cultivate the land or maybe it was simply a question of funds, but in any event it was decided that we should leave London where housing was impossible to find and move to the countryside, somewhere near enough to allow my father to commute to London.

I have no idea how he was to find and buy Innes House, in Wickford, Essex. It was isolated in its four acres of abandoned uncultivated land, somewhere in the middle of no-mans land, two or three miles from the railway station. It was a mile and a half or so from a paved road and the access to it was by way of what was then described as an unmade road - a cart-track in the mud which led through fields. The grounds held three small apple orchards, overgrown and abandoned, but not without a certain old English charm. The house itself was an enigma. A house with all the rooms having the right names, scullery, pantry, breakfast room, but somehow lacking the essentials like a proper bathroom, sanitation, kitchen, and worst of all, electricity.

Almost unnoticed, we moved back into the early nineteenth century, but this time, without domestic help. My father appeared to take to this with total equanimity. I suspect that my mother was somewhat nonplussed but she remained stoic.

The move with our pathetic belongings was not without complications. We were happy to escape from Muswell Hill but a little apprehensive of what Wickford held in store. Naturally it rained on the day we moved in the autumn of 1947. All went reasonably well until we reached the unmade road leading to our house. The removal lorry, with some persuasion from us, inched forward in a bold attempt to reach the house but was immediately bogged down to the axles in mud. After an hour or so, with the aid of branches cut from the hedge, the driver was able to retreat and extricate the lorry from the mud. Furious, he then set about discharging all our belongings into the mud and left us standing in the rain with the night drawing in. My father disappeared and returned half an hour later with a wheelbarrow to transport a few essentials which he had manage to borrow from a local farm. It was arranged with the farmer that he would, next day, transport the rest of our belongings to the house with the aid of his tractor. It took us two days to move in, clean off the mud and get more or less organised. Oil lamps were the thing. They took a bit of getting used to, smoked like hell in the draft and gave off choking fumes. To start with we had a single hurricane lantern but quickly graduated to Tilley lamps which when adjusted, gave a light almost as good as electricity.

In due course we modernised. A bathroom was installed and proper sanitation. Gas was put in and of course, electricity. It was still a rambling barn of a house with fireplaces that smoked like hell when the wind was from the east.

Working on the assumption that digging was good for you, Father commenced digging like mad, shaping up vegetable beds and planting fruit bushes. We bought and raised geese, ducks and chickens together with goats which my mother and Maureen milked each day. All these things gave not much time for amusement. A far cry from life as we used to know it in Monte Carlo. We had become smallholders in Essex.

My father duly became manager of a prestigious bank in Pall Mall and each working day rose at the crack of dawn to walk a couple of miles to the railway station to catch the train for London. He returned each night at about eight o'clock having to walk back all the way from the station. He dined, and then went out to dig in the light of a hurricane lamp. A page had turned in his life and Monte Carlo and its sophisticated social life no longer existed. My mother, who was susceptible to the finer things of life, art, literature, music now spoke mainly to her geese, ducks and goats. The fortunes of war. She never showed that she was unhappy and maintained a stoic attitude to life, looking after us and making sure that our education did not want.

Speaking of education, on arriving at Wickford, we were found schools, Maureen went to a convent in Brentwood and I to a school in Chelmsford. From the first, Maureen hated her school and particularly the uniform she was obliged to wear which was mud brown with purple stripes. Thick brown stockings, and no nonsense stout brown shoes. The nuns imposed a harsh discipline which didn't help and Maureen took an instant dislike to most of her fellow pupils; girls who didn't have to milk goats before going to school. For other reasons, I also loathed my school, some six hundred boys selected to enter careers in the Army. Once more I found myself in a rigid school, with the customary morning assembly and the usual obligatory prayers. The school hall, all panelled oak and stained glass windows, contained the names of the boys who had fallen to the glory of the country and their school in the Great War and Second World War.

Chapter 13

Perhaps the most difficult period of my youth commenced with the move to Wickford and subsequent schooling at Chelmsford. The primitive condition under which we lived in the home were hard to start with before the house was modernised. Other than for one or two friends at school who were far from close, I thought myself cut off from the world. One escape was my frequent visits to the public library where a selection of yachting magazines were available. These would provide me with dreams of boats and offered a means of temporary escape. None of my few friends shared this passion for the sea.

The turning point arrived during the spring of 1950 after a argument with my father which ended with my being told acidly that I would never leave my mother's apron strings. My father nevertheless proposed a test. He suggested that I should enter the British Merchant navy as an apprentice officer.

As I now look back, he must have already prepared the ground with his good friend Richardson. It turned out that one of Richardson's close friends owned a cargo ship capable of having one or two cadet officers on board. As it happened, their one and only cadet officer was due to complete his time at the end of summer 1950 and his place would be available for me should my father wish to reserve it for me.

My biggest problem was my maths. I had always favoured a rather approximate method which didn't always agree with the accepted rules of theory. It was clear by now that this subject was to be an essential part of my future life. My notion of approximate arithmetic, geometry and algebra was to have to take on an altogether different meaning. In the months left before the end of the school year and the exams, I set to and revised my attitude to maths.

No one was more amazed than me when the results of the examinations came through and I had passed. The way ahead was clear. It was now up to my father, who was as surprised as me, but pleased. He immediately contacted Richardson's friend. It seemed that the company, the Sundale Shipping Company Ltd., was willing to accept me, subject of course to an interview at the head office in St Helen's Place, London.

In the meantime, I had received a letter from Robert, the officer who had just completed his time with Sundale, saying that it would be nice if we could meet and talk about life at sea. He came to see me in Wickford. He described my future occupations and made amusing remarks covering the conditions of life on board his ex-ship, the *Sunbridge*. He brought with him a few manuals of basic seamanship and navigation and most useful of all, a complete list of clothing, uniforms and gear that I would need.

Maybe I should have been a little more attentive to what he was saying and in particular to the reason why he was abandoning the sea for a career as a civil airline pilot! (We had occasion to meet in London, two or three years later and he admitted then that life on board the *Sunbridge* had not been particularly inspiring and that he had avoided at the time of our meeting in Wickford mentioning any negative aspects which might have caused me to worry). His visit left me fired with enthusiasm but mixed with a small dose of apprehension when faced with the actual reality of things. I had read many of Joseph Conrad's books and instinctively felt that perhaps life at sea was not necessarily all a bed of roses. Some thorns poking up through the mattress perhaps.

Arrangements were made for me to travel to London in the company of my father to meet the ship owner's director during the course of the first week of October 1950. It was my first visit in an office in the City. I was amazed. It was Dickensian, dark and forbidding. The manager, an austere man, didn't exactly inspire me and reminded me of my old headmaster who had soundly beaten my backside a few years before. Our reception was cool. I had the impression that he doubted my ability to last out the prescribe four years of sea service. However, I was told that I would be accepted subject to a medical examination.

The next step therefore was the unavoidable Board of Trade medical examination. Accompanied by my mother, I duly presented myself at the surgery of the Board of Trade doctor in London where I underwent a somewhat perfunctory examination and was passed fit for service. This was followed immediately by an eyesight test at the Merchant Navy examination centre in Dock Street, East London. The examiner was a Welshman; the official Board of Trade examiner for Masters & Mates.

He was a man totally devoid of a sense of humour. I was suffering from a bad cold at the time and perhaps this did not help in his initial attitude towards me. Also, I had difficulty in coming to terms with his broad Welsh accent which was totally foreign to my ears.

The interview started badly when, without thinking I corrected his pronunciation of my name. This was unforgivable. He marched me into a completely darkened room where a sort of lantern-slide projector and screen, had been set up. He told me that he would show me a succession of pinpricks of light, two at a time, side by side, of colours red, green and white - obviously navigation lights. My trouble was that I had never seen a white light. To me lights which weren't coloured were yellow, some sort of throw back to oil lamps, I suspect.

We started but very quickly came to a halt when the Welsh voice from the dark barked at me that what I had just seen was white and not yellow. We resumed; seconds later, there was a shout - "Idiot, white, not yellow!" By this time, I was in a state of nerves, my nose all blocked up and my eyes running with strain. I was beginning to have serious thoughts on the advisability of going to sea. He started again, flashing the lights as fast as he could go. I could barely keep up and inevitably, "yellow" came out again. Everything came to a grinding halt. The lights came on and the examiner said "Boyo, (the first but not the last, time that I was to hear this expression) you are not only blind but deaf as well - go home!" With that he scribbled out a certificate to the effect that my colour vision was defective and that I was unfit for service at sea.

Crushed and shocked at this turn of events, I returned to Wickford, unable to understand fully what had happened. It was evident that I was not colour blind, nor did I have any other defects with regard to vision, yet the certificate clearly stated that my eyesight was defective. My ambition lay in ruins because of a short tempered examiner whom I had dared to correct his mispronunciation of my name.

Seriously upset, I decided that since I could not go to sea, my other interest lay in architecture and particularly in the restoration of ancient monuments, cathedrals and the like. Close by in the seaside town of Southend there existed a technical college where one could read architecture - a five year course. I recall. So without losing any time, I presented myself, was interviewed and duly enrolled. It occurred to me that since I was said to be colour blind, this affliction would not necessarily be very helpful in architecture either. An architect unable to see a white light was likely to be suspect.

The more my parents thought about it, the more it seemed that the Board of Trade eyesight test results were ridiculous. With a feeling of having been unjustly treated, my parents wrote to the principal examiner of the Board of Trade in London and appealed against the results. They duly received a reply to the effect that in the event that it could be proved that my eyesight was not defective, they might consider re-examining me. This, then, required a visit to an eye specialist. Accordingly, it was arranged that I should be seen by a specialist in Moorefields Eye Hospital in London. My eyesight was examined from all angles but not once was I asked to describe a white light. I passed the tests with flying colours so to speak and armed with a certificate from one of the foremost leading eye specialist in London, the Board of Trade duly accepted to re-examine me.

With certain trepidation, I returned to Dock Street in London. This time I had no cold. The same Welshman, the same mispronunciation of my name, but this time, no correction on my part. Saw not a glimmer of a yellow light whatsoever and passed the test. I was to meet the same examiner some four years later when he examined me for the oral part of the examination for Second Mates certificate. He remembered my name and still mispronounced it! By that time though, I had become somewhat fireproof against this sort of thing.

Chapter 14

Having passed the medical tests, I was ready to join the company. I cancelled my architectural course and the day came when my mother and I took the train for London to buy my uniforms which my parents had very generously arranged to pay for.

We made our way to Limehouse in East London to the naval outfitters to which I had been directed by the company. The location Gardiners Corner still exists although the store which formed an angle between East India Dock road and West India Dock road was demolished some years ago. To me, it was like Aladdin's cave. Gardiner sold everything from kit bags, sea boots, oilskins to uniforms and greatcoats. Armed with Robert's list and with the aid of an assistant we worked our way through the various departments amassing a huge pile of clothing ranging from tropical kit through to working gear in the form of dungarees, as jeans were called in those days. The most awkward item to deal with and pack was the oilskin, a full length job, as worn by the Cape Horners. Black, sticky and evil smelling but said to be indispensable. In fact I very rarely wore it throughout the four years I spent on board the *Sunbridge*. It hung in the back of my locker, gradually melting into a formless shape like stick of half eaten liquorice. When I left the ship it was welded to the back of the locker where, I presume, it remained until the ship was broken up.

My proudest moment of the day however, was when I tried on my dress uniform and greatcoat, splendid with bright brass buttons. Other than for admirals and staff officers, I doubt very much now if a greatcoat forms part of the current naval officer's wardrobe, but at that time, or so the shop assistant told us, it was a necessary part of the uniform. It was to come in useful later on in my career. I wore it but very rarely on the *Sunbridge* for fear of getting it dirty and in the event that none of the other officers on the *Sunbridge* possessed such a luxurious coat, it was better that it should remain hidden discreetly in my wardrobe. Thick white roll-neck sweaters and battle-dress were going to be the rig of the day - other than when I was in dungarees, which, as it turned out, was most of the time!

Within a few days following our shopping expedition, I received instructions from Sundale to join their vessel, in Newport, South Wales, on the 20th October 1950. My contract in the form of the traditional indentures arrived at the same time for signature.

This imposing document in linen and sporting an enormous red Common Seal of the Company, set down the articles under which I would be trained. The terms were those which were probably used for the same purpose in the eighteenth century. My father " *hereinafter called the Surety",* and I signed this awesome document in which:

"the said Alex Sinclair hereby voluntarily binds himself Apprentice unto the said Company and their Assigns, for the term of four years.....and pay the said Apprentice the sum of £390 in the following manner...for the first years' service seventy-five pounds, for the second years' service ninety pounds, for the third years' service £105 and for the fourth years' service £120, ...and twelve shillings yearly in lieu of washing".

For sake of comparison a deck boy, in those days earned a maximum of £ 84 per year. So, after the first year, I would be better off than him. Great news.

Chapter 15

The morning of the 20th October dawned cold and wet, I was sixteen years old. Dressed in my splendid new uniform, greatcoat, cap and gloves, but wearing wellyboots to keep my shoes clean of mud, I was accompanied by my family who helped me with my kit bag and trunk to Wickford station to catch the early morning train to London. I changed into shoes and suddenly realised that I didn't know precisely where I was going. Nor did I know when I should be back. An emotional and very apprehensive parting. My uniform bolstered my courage and by the time I had caught the train at Paddington Station for Newport, I was quite cheerful having accomplished what I thought then would be the most difficult part of the journey.

It was beginning to get dark by the time the train pulled into Newport station. Not many passengers descended but by the time I had managed to drag my trunk and kit bag out of the compartment all the porters (those were the days) had disappeared. Not a good start. It was to get worse. Having arrived outside the station at the taxi-rank, there was not a taxi in sight and I was all alone. It was raining and a cold, wet wind was blowing in off the Bristol Channel. My new uniform was getting wet and I was worried that I should not be able to present myself on board in a properly dignified manner. After standing around for about what seemed to be an eternity, I was amazed to see a Rolls Royce pull up alongside me. This was my taxi. Even though the car was of pre-war vintage, it was still impressive. Things were looking up. I gave the driver the name of the ship and was surprised to learn that he knew where to find her.

Newport that afternoon was not impressive. The overall picture of black coal tips, dreary, mean terraced houses and the absence of people in the rain soaked streets did nothing to encourage my apprehensive mood despite the Rolls Royce. The docks were even worse. Never in my life had I ever set foot in an industrial zone. Cranes, rusting hangars, conveyors and machinery lay all around in the semi-darkness in what appeared to me to be like a battle field after the battle.

Finally we arrived alongside a grey, dirty administrative building. Ahead of us, I caught sight of my first glimpse of the *Sunbridge*. Strangely, she seemed to have sunk into the ground with only the masts, funnel and part of the superstructure visible from where I sat. I climbed out of my Rolls reluctantly and struggled with my gear to the foot of a filthy broken-down wooden gangway leading down onto the main deck. The place was deserted in the rain, with barely enough light to see where I was going. I was astonished to see that the vessel lay in drydock, something which I had never even thought about. Unaided, slipping and sliding on the wet gangway, I managed to get my gear down onto the deck.

Before I had time to take stock of my surroundings, I became aware of a person on the forward boat deck, sheltering from the rain beneath the wing of the bridge. It was apparent that he had been there for some time and had seen me getting out of the Rolls. He stood there looking down at me without saying anything. We stood looking at each other for a while before I felt that in view of his silence, I should introduce myself. With rain dripping down from my cap, I told him who I was in the hope that I was not making a big mistake for, after all, I had not actually seen the name of the ship written anywhere. Still he said nothing but turned around and disappeared into the accommodation to reappear in the doorway of the bridge accommodation on the main deck. He was middle-aged, fat with a big beer-belly hanging over the top of his trousers. He was dressed in a worn and stained battle-dress top and grey flannel trousers; he wore the epaulettes of a chief officer. His appearance shocked me, but this was only the first of the shocks I was to receive before the day was out.

"I know who you are boyo", he said with a strong Welsh accent *"Now you get out of that fancy dress you're wearing. Put on your dungarees and come back to see me".* Second big, big, shock! Welsh, distinctly unpleasant in manner and here again was this "boyo" business.

By this time he had been joined by a stocky youngish looking chap in civvies with an exceptionally large hook nose and small piercing eyes. No doubt he took pity on me since he kindly offered to help me get my luggage to the cabin that had been allotted to me. He introduced himself as Mickey, the second steward who doubled up as the Captain's personal servant. He helped me unpack and showed me where and how to stow my gear. He told me to charge quickly into working gear and boots and gave me directions to the chief officer's cabin. As an aside he told me that the toilets on board could not be used since hey emptied out over the side into the drydock! These, however, could be found ashore.

Having carefully put my new clothes away and now dressed in my white sweater, dungarees and boots, I found my way to the Chief Officer's cabin. Without any preamble he told me to get a scrubbing brush, mop, bucket and go swab (wash) out the seamen's mess-room. Fortunately, Mickey, who had been hovering in the alleyway outside had overhead the order and was able to translate all this in terms of obtaining the necessary equipment and showing me the way to the mess-room, right aft in the bowels of the ship. By this time night had fallen, it was still raining and blowing a gale from the south west and I was wishing I was back at home in front of the fire listening to the adventures of Paul Temple, detective, on the radio.

Horror of horrors! The mess room was flooded with stagnant, filthy water coming from a defective drain from the crew showers. It was obvious that it had lain there for several days since the crew had not yet joined the ship and the whole place was cold and deserted. Left alone to my own devices and not having much of a clue as to how to go about swabbing out, I first used the bucket to bale out. I guessed that it was forbidden to throw anything overboard in the dry dock. It occurred to me then that it being night and raining, no one would see me throwing buckets of dirty water down into the dry dock. I had accurately seized the intentions of the chief officer to get rid of the water without calling in costly labour. Struggling up and down the companionway leading from the deck down into the mess-room, I worked almost in the dark alone for a couple of hours before Mickey rescued me and took me to the engineer officers' mess room where he had cooked for me some bacon, sausages and eggs. The bread was stale and the bacon and sausages were tainted but at least it was something to eat. I returned to my task and duly completed swabbing out sometime after midnight. Since there was no water available on board, I couldn't wash and went to bed as I was. I had never been so exhausted in my life.

So ended my first day aboard the *Sunbridge*. With certain satisfaction, when all was finished, I peed over the side into the dry dock.

Ever since then, the 20th of October has been a very special day for me. I shall never forget the smell of that stagnant, putrid water (I didn't smell too good myself either), nor will I ever forget the taste of those tainted sausages.

The following day dawned bright with a brisk south-westerly wind from the sea. I was woken by Mickey at seven thirty who hold me that I had best get back into my working gear and come to the officer's pantry to get some breakfast. The loos, he told me again were ashore, on the quayside adjacent to the dry-dock, but there was no water for me to wash in for the time being. First things first, I thought, and decided to visit the loos. I scrambled up the gangway and had no trouble in locating the building, the proverbial brick shit-house. Luckily I wore my wellyboots - believe me, I needed them. There was not a stall where the door was not either totally missing or hanging off its hinges. It was foul; not a good start to the day.

From then on, for several days, until the seagoing crew arrived, I was given all the most menial jobs on deck. Sweeping and cleaning up after the thousand and one repairs that were being carried out by riggers and maintenance engineers. The noise of riveting echoed throughout the ship accompanied by shouts and abuse in a foul language the meaning of which I could only guess! My relationship with William, the chief officer, remained cold. I learnt later he had been told that my family were friends of the ship-owner. Not entirely correct but, somewhere along the grapevine, he must have heard something about the circumstances of my being accepted by the company. Arriving in a Rolls Royce hadn't helped either. Fortunately, he lived nearby in Cardiff and went home each afternoon, leaving me in peace but in the hands of the bosun whose one idea was to work me into the deck. Mickey told me that

William had told the bosun that I was a fancy boyo needing to be shaped up. Couldn't argue with that, I suppose.

Needless to say I was never out of my working dungarees and sea boots, which, by the time the crew arrived were in a sad and sorry state. I washed, more or less, out of a bucket which at night I secretly emptied into the drydock. Food was something which nobody around me seemed to care for. A slice of corned-beef (which I carefully extracted and threw away) between two slabs of stale bread and butter comprised lunch each day and a fry-up of tainted sausages and eggs cooked by Mickey served as tea. This culinary feast was served in the engineer's grubby mess-room, shared in company of a couple of Welsh engineers in dirty boiler-suits who ignored me completely and whose sole topic of conversation, so far as I could decipher, related apparently to mysterious bits of ironmongery called bearings, liners, valves and con-rods.

On the matter of technicalities, this leads me to think that perhaps a description of my new home the Sunbridge at this stage might be helpful to those not having had the good fortune to serve at sea in antique vessels.

The *Sunbridge* had been built in Kowloon, Hong-Kong, in 1938. She was a cargo ship of riveted construction modelled along traditional lines of design for ships which had existed since the turn of the century. The bridge and officer's accommodation were located between cargo holds N. 2 and 3. The engine, boiler room together with the engineers and petty officers accommodation and galley were between holds numbers 3 and 4. Aft of the last hold, number 5, was the crew accommodation which housed both the seamen, engine-room oilers or firemen and donkey man together with the mess-room. The accommodation had been extended during the war to house the army artillery crew who manned the 4 inch gun. Aft of the accommodation was the ammunition locker. At the time I sailed on her, the crew numbered 12 officers and petty officers and about 25 seamen, deck and cabin boys and engine-room oilers. Immediately prior to my arrival on board she had also carried a complement of about a dozen stokers who fed the boilers with coal. A few months previously however, she had been converted from coal burning to oil, so the stokers were no longer required.

The ship was powered by a triple-expansion (3 cylinders - small, medium and large !) steam-engine capable or propelling her in loaded condition at a speed of about 9 knots in fine weather and calm sea. In any sort of heavy weather she would drop back to 6 knots; not exactly an ocean greyhound. The galley ovens were fired by coal. I mention this because I was told, soon after I joined the ship, that I was responsible for the coal, or more accurately, it was me that humped the twenty-five kilo bags of coal on my back from lorries ashore to the coal-bunkers on board (three hours works. In addition to my other responsibilities, I thus became a coal-man).

Although, so far as my own living quarters were concerned, I was classed officially as an officer, there was no room for me in the officers' accommodation beneath the bridge. I was accommodated in a cabin tucked in between that of the cooks and the Fourth Engineer in the starboard working-alleyway of the engine-room accommodation. Two portholes looked out onto the weather-deck alleyway beneath the boat deck which provided some shelter in bad weather and shade in the tropics. The bulkheads were of polished mahogany, equipped with brass fittings. Bunk, settee, wardrobe, locker, fold-down table beneath a bookshelf and small sink with running hot and cold water completed the furnishings. The deck, as was the inside working alleyway, was of traditional teak planking. Although my room was very narrow and small, it was my place of refuge and in the years to come. I was to grow quite fond of it. Even the old leaking steam radiator with asbestos lagging had a charm of sorts.

Chapter 16

Shortly after my arrival, the greater part of the repair work had been completed. The painting gangs overside were putting the final touches to the hull which was coloured in black with the customary red anti-foul. Stores were brought alongside. Frozen meat, eggs, cartons of canned food and fresh vegetables together with dry stores and paint arrived in profusion.

A couple of days before we were due to leave Newport, the new seagoing crew arrived. The deck crew and officers were Welsh, with the exception of the Second Officer, whilst the engine-room oilers were Somalis. The donkey-man was Yemeni. The two cooks, my immediate neighbours, however, were Nigerian and the chief was a fat, arrogant little man who was to cause me a lot of trouble later. We loathed each other on first sight! Unfortunately I was to share the same feeling for the Chief Steward who was part of the permanent crew. He was exceedingly lumpy having been a professional weightlifter before the war and had gone terribly to seed. Hovering in the background was a lad of my age, the cabin boy. The poor lad was slow and useless but nevertheless, with Mickey, made up the numbers of the catering department.

The engineers comprised a strange and bewildering mixture of humanity. The Chief engineer was a huge mountain of fat, so gross that I doubted that he would be able to go down the engine-room ladders. He possessed only one blue serge suit with a Fremlins Brown Ale badge (little elephant) in his lapel. Later his sole concession to the tropics was to remove his jacket, collar and tie. For all his unfortunate appearance, he was a kind man and always treated me with courtesy. The second engineer was from Leith in Scotland. An alcoholic, with a permanent dose of the shakes. He had suffered badly during the war but was nevertheless, apparently, an excellent engineer who kept the *Sunbridge* running. He, together with the fourth engineer, a young, capable officer (my other neighbour) was almost entirely responsible to the good maintenance of the engine. Like most of the others, the fourth engineer was from South Wales but had been too young to serve at sea during the war. He had been runner up to the South Wales lightweight boxing championships and was useful later in teaching me how to defend myself. The last of the engineers was the third, who, in addition to his watch keeping duties, doubled up as electrician. This poor man was totally punch-drunk. He had been a Royal Navy boxing champion during the war; I now forget in which category. His nose was squashed flat against his face and his cauliflower ears jutted out monstrously from the side of his head. He had been so knocked about that even his eyesight was poor and without his round, wire- rimmed glasses, he could see almost nothing (half way through the first voyage he was to tread on his glasses and from then on lived in a twilight zone).

The Second Officer was something altogether different. He was Estonian and had served in the Russian navy during the war with the rank of commander. He had somehow managed to get to England via Finland and Sweden, but how he ended up serving on the *Sunbridge* is a mystery. It must be remembered that at that time Britain had the biggest merchant fleet in the world and had lost so many ships, officers and men during the war that it was difficult to fill all the posts. The Estonian's English appeared to be very limited and in any event he spoke to absolutely no one other than for those few words essential for the job. He wore his old naval uniform stripped of rank insignia and like the chief engineer, seemed to have no other clothes. His baggage comprised a sextant and an accordion. He refused to use electric light in his cabin. In those days, each of the officer's cabin was equipped with a brass oil lamp and it was with this that he lit his room. Later, when off watch at night at sea, he was to lock his cabin and play the accordion, singing what may have been sad, nostalgic Estonian folk songs to himself. One could only guess at what he had seen during the war which had deranged him. In any event, if possible, I gave him a wide berth.

The Third Officer, another Welshman, had served in the Royal Navy during the war as skipper of small supply vessels, delivering stores to coastal defence positions in the Bristol Channel. By all accounts his war had been a quiet one. He now sported a thin hairline moustache which gave him, irrespective of the uniform he wore, the appearance of a spiv.

The Wireless Officer was relatively young but seldom mixed with anybody and looked through me as though I didn't exist.

William, who seemed to hold me in such low esteem, was the chief officer. His thing was spitting on the deck between his feet and chain-smoking. Throughout the four years we sailed together, I can't say that I got to know him. I never found out anything about his life other than I think that he had been in command during the war and had somehow lost it. He was the only one amongst all the other officers who appeared to be married although I never saw his wife. I don't know if he had any children. A taciturn man who mixed with no one other than with the Captain.

The Captain, or "Old Man" as he was always referred to, was, probably, when I think back, the only more or less "normal" person on board. Married with a son and daughter, he lived in Cardiff. I think that William must have told him that I was on board but I had no contact with him during those few days before we sailed from Newport. Dressed permanently in dungarees and boots, I still ate my meals in the pantry and had no access to the dining saloon.

Chapter 17

The morning of the 2nd November 1950 dawned bright but with a strong westerly wind. As usual I was on deck at eight o'clock but having no specific job, I stood around looking at others working as the crew secured the hatches and dropped the derricks, tasks I was incapable of taking part in because of the lack of knowing what it was all about. I watched the dry-dock slowly filling with water on which all sorts of rubbish floated - bits and pieces which had fallen into the dock during the last couple of weeks. The dock gates were opened when the level in the dock reached that of water outside and two tugs took our mooring ropes aft and towed us out of the dock stern first. Lunch had been served early, at 11 o'clock on account of tide and the departure manoeuvres which were likely to last for over a couple of hours.

I had written to my parents telling them that we would be going to London to load a general cargo destined for Australia. The letter had been posted by Mickey on one of his solitary expeditions ashore at night.

The wind was blowing strongly and it was cold. The sky was covered in a chaotic mass of grey and white clouds which were occasionally torn apart to reveal a small patch of blue sky and a ray of pale sunshine. The wind smelt clean and salty, a real change from the few days previously when the air had been filled the smell of coal smoke, smog and wet coal. We turned around and passed out through the locks heading into the channel leading to the Bristol Channel, a few miles away. The tugs were let go and at last we were on our way.

A great billowing pall of black smoke issued from our tall, thin funnel which was painted in the company livery of fine raspberry red with a narrow white band beneath a black top.

By the time that we had cleared the river channel and entered the Bristol channel it was mid-afternoon. The wind had strengthened and the sun, by now, had totally disappeared leaving the surrounding sea the colour of lead, flecked with white caps.

Up until that moment I had been congratulating myself that no one seemed to have taken an interest in me. William had told me previously that he would have me on his watch, that is to say the four to eight (four to eight o'clock in the morning and the same again in the evening). I had been quite pleased at this idea, thinking that this would leave me the greater part of the day free to study and do whatever I liked. Also, the thought of being on watch with the Estonian "admiral" as he became known, or with the Third Officer didn't altogether fill me with enthusiasm.

Convinced that I would not be required until four o'clock that afternoon, I had changed out of grubby dungarees into a clean white shirt, tie and my new battle-dress uniform complete with epaulettes of rank. Nice, but a little premature. It was about two-thirty in the afternoon when the bosun found me. Perhaps a little more crudely than I thought necessary, he thrust a shovel into my hand and informed me that I was to shovel over the side the huge pile of galley garbage and ashes from the galley stoves. This mountain of rotting galley garbage, ash and clinker lay on the starboard side of N4 hatchway, next to the galley. I had passed by this evil smelling heap each day in Newport and had wondered why it had remained on deck and had not be collected by refuse collectors. Now, I knew! This was going to be really nasty.

As I said, this mountain of garbage lay on the starboard side, close to the galley. This is relevant unfortunately because the vessel was heading out into the Atlantic on a south-westerly course and the "weather side", that is to say the side from which the wind was blowing was the starboard side. It doesn't take a lot of imagination to realise that as I shovelled it over the side, half of it would fly back up on board with a vengeance and hit me in the face.

By the time I started to shovel, the deck crew had disappeared down below and I was left alone with my task to cope as best I could. As night fell no one came to relieve me to see how I was getting on. Worse still, I became aware that the wind had strengthened and that the sea was now quite rough. So rough, in fact, that as the ship pitched down into a trough, the propeller came out of the water. Not only was she pitching up and down like a roller-coaster, but she was starting to roll over heavily to each side making my job even more difficult.

I had no experience of standing on the heaving deck of a ship heading out into an Atlantic storm. By the time it was dark, I was wet through, covered from head to foot in ash and garbage and in the grips of seasickness. I do not know where my hidden resistance came from (I had certainly never ever had the occasion to call upon it before) but I finally completed the job some before midnight. I crawled to the shower I shared with the cooks, cleaned up, but not knowing what to do with my stinking clothes, I left them in a pile in a corner of the shower room: this, needless to say, was to bring me trouble from the cook in the morning.

I was woken up by a seaman banging on my door saying that it was "one bell", quarter to four in the morning and I was needed on the bridge. If anything, the movement of the ship was worse, although the wind had lessened and the sky was clear. As I made my way up to the bridge my feeling of nausea returned. Somehow I managed to keep it under control. In any event, after having spent so many hours shovelling garbage, the air at four o'clock in the morning smelt of the sea, clean and fresh. I climbed up the accommodation ladders, past the Old Man's deck onto the bridge and into the wheelhouse. The brass work, which I had polished during our stay in Newport, gleamed in the subdued lamplight of the compass binnacle. It was warm inside, but already William had his cigarette going and the smoke did nothing to help my nausea.

Although there was the customary lookout posted forward, on the foc'le head, I was told by William that since I was fit for nothing, I might as well go up on the upper bridge known as the "monkey-island" and be a lookout. I was to advise him of the presence of other ships on the horizon by using the voice pipe that connected the upper, or standard compass with that in the wheelhouse.

It was now that my experience in London with the lantern-slide show could come in useful; white, not yellow light. The monkey-island was, of course, open to the elements and although the wind had dropped slightly, it was still beastly cold up there. Up high, the movement of the ship was accentuated and it was all that I could do to prevent myself from being sick. For a short while I managed to call down to the wheelhouse the presence of other ships around us and then decided that since the "real" lookouts were there anyway, and had probably reported the same presence of the same ships that I had seen, I would take the weight off my feet and sit down on some wireless office battery boxes. Still exhausted and feeling sea sick, it was not long, before the inevitable happened and I fell asleep.

At some stage I must have slipped off the battery box onto the deck. I was brutally awakened by the chief officer who was evidently trying to kick me to death. Fortunately being well wrapped up in a thick sweater and oil skins I suffered no permanent damage. My self-esteem however, had taken a knock. William was yelling at me furiously. I would have been shot at dawn had we still been at war.

It seemed to me that life at sea was not all that it had been cracked to be. By chance I had escaped, being killed by Italian torpedoes and German bombs. I thought it now a bit exaggerated on the part of William, to want to shoot me. I was thoroughly miserable and cold by the time I left the bridge at eight o'clock that morning.

My feeling of sickness had passed though, and although I have no further recollections of the passage to London, I must have performed my looking-out business with due diligence. I found out, to my dismay, that after my morning watch and a piece of toast for breakfast (still in the pantry), I was required to work on deck with the day working sailors and given the same menial tasks as those of the deck-boy. The only difference was that the boy did not have to get up and be on watch at four in the morning, nor was he on duty until eight at night. That remained my privilege.

We arrived in London and berthed alongside King George V dock. For the first time I was able to see the big ships of prestigious companies, Cunard, Union-Castle, British India, P & O and others. Although not the only one, we were, by comparison, like something out of the past, a relic of the pre-war. There were so many ships that some were double banked on one side. The adjacent Royal Albert dock and Victoria dock were the same, filled with vessels, all flying the Red Ensign ; an impressive sight.

Immediately after our arrival I was called to the Old Man's cabin where I was formally introduced and given a lecture on my inadmissible behaviour on watch for having fallen asleep. This was not to be tolerated, he said, and like any schoolboy, I was threatened with expulsion should it ever occur again. By then, I was seriously reconsidering my future and felt like returning to college to study architecture. I felt, though, that after all the expense my parents had gone to in buying uniforms and gear, I couldn't let them down. I firmly resolved never to be in such a position again whereby I could be criticised and, to hell with it, I would continue right to the end, even if it killed me. Although I was only sixteen, I think probably that it was the day I left behind me my childhood. I would no longer be frightened if I was sworn at, and would grin and bear it.

Chapter 18

I have no vivid recollection of the stay in London other than for one weekend when I was allowed to return to Wickford to see my family. I put on my best uniform and greatcoat and caught the train from Liverpool Street station. The mere fact of climbing out of my dungarees and dressing up in my uniform bolstered my morale. I did not, of course, tell my parents of my experiences on board, but let them know that I was living the life of an officer and gentleman ; more or less anyway.

It transpired that we were loading a full cargo of general merchandise, some 8000 tons, for various ports in Australia. Although I knew nothing about the stowage and lashing of cargo, I was sent into the holds as "watchman" to prevent the dockers from broaching and pilfering from the cases and cartons which were being loaded.

My first contact with dockers was not a happy one. My attempts at being some sort of policeman were, needless to say fairly disastrous, and I leave it to the imagination what the results of a confrontation between burly foul-mouthed London dockers and a cadet officer just out of school was like. Even then, it was not beyond the realms of my understanding that my presence in the holds was not necessarily one of theft prevention but was part of the general scheme of getting me "Shaped Up".

Loading completed, we duly sailed from London, on the 23rd November 1950, bound for Adelaide via Cape Town and the Cape of Good Hope. Late November in the English Channel and the Bay of Biscay was hardly a pleasure. We were low in the water and most of the time, the weather-deck was awash. On leaving London, I was again shovelling shit for want of a better word, but this time I was not alone. The day-work sailors were mobilised and it was over and done with quite quickly. In any event, the garbage had not lain on the deck for weeks, rotting and festering as it had done in Newport. I was no longer suffering from seasickness and was getting acclimatised to standing on the monkey-island, appropriately named I thought, exposed to the wind and rain, part of the night and day.

By the time we were passing Cap Finisterre, the weather had improved and I had begun to enjoy this time on the monkey island where no one bothered me; not that anybody actually talked to me other than for giving me orders. At about this time however, lookouts were dispensed with and I became a redundant lookout. William then couldn't have me just standing around doing nothing so I was seriously put to polishing brass and scrubbing the wheel-house deck when it became sufficiently light to do so. This was of limited productivity, so I was quickly formed to take over from the seaman on the wheel and taught to steer. William discovered that I had a natural aptitude for helming and very quickly I was to take the place of one seaman on the four to eight watch.

My position on watch was then assured and lasted throughout the four years I was to remain on the *Sunbridge*. In fact, I was to become the star helmsman and took over the wheel whenever there was a pilot on board or when manoeuvring became tricky in confined waters, whatever the time of day or night.

On passing the equator for the first time and in accordance with the custom, the sailors cornered me and plastered me with galley slops (the slops bit was not actually part of the substance usually utilised which was normally a flour and water paste). Not having a great sense of humour and unable to appreciate the moment, I attacked my tormentors with murderous intent, inflicting some random pain before I was eventually brought down and sat on. My performance earned the name of "Freddy the Fearless Fly" after a character in the then popular boy's Dandy Comic; thereafter I was known as Freddy - perhaps an advantage over being just "hey-boyo!"

My relationship with the Nigerian cook was not good. Not only was he a lousy cook, he was also a surly, arrogant bully, the likes of which we see occasionally on television in some poor knocked about central African state, dressed in a general's uniform. It had been ordered by William that I should be responsible for the cleanliness of the starboard working-alleyway leading through the engineer's accommodation. It had also been agreed that since not only did it pass in front of my cabin, it also passed in front of the cooks' cabin and therefore the duty of scrubbing the alleyway should fall to the cooks as well as myself. The second cook, also Nigerian, was a friendly, meek and mild elderly man with gold rimmed glasses, gold teeth and a mop of white hair who, in all fairness, was incapable of getting on his hands and knees and scrubbing decks. His strong point, at which he excelled, was peeling spuds.

This was my Saturday afternoon job. The cook told me that he was cook and not deck-boy: scrubbing decks was the job of deck-boys and that was that; no discussion. I had no option but to get on with it. Now, added to this was another factor which made my life difficult and which also lasted four years. On the other side of the alleyway, opposite my door, was the access door to the engine-room. Not only was it used by the Third and Fourth engineers, but also by the Arab donkey-man and oilers. Because of their oily boots, I had asked them to use the stokehold entrance to the engine-room on the weather-deck, but needless to say, even after having complained to the chief engineer, they continued to use the alleyway leaving the imprints of their oily boots on my cleanly scrubbed teak deck. I mention this because later, this ongoing battle with the donkey-man led him to attack me with a butcher's knife borrowed from the galley. Also, it did nothing to enhance relationship with the junior engineers whose boots were no cleaner than those of the donkey man and who cared little for my problem of keeping the deck clean.

The captain, chief officer and chief steward, notebook in hand, would make a tour of inspection of all the accommodation each Sunday morning at 11 o'clock whilst at sea. This was a ritual. Each cabin, shower and toilet was inspected in turn and, if found by the captain to be not properly cleaned, the fact would be recorded in the inspection log and the responsible reprimanded. This was a weekly source of aggravation which lasted years since "my" alleyway always showed black footmarks leading from the engine-room to the weather-deck.

In my spare time, if I was ever to be allowed to have any, I was supposed to study. I had a yearly syllabus which covered maths, physics, navigation and seamanship. At the end of each year, I had to sit a Board of Trade examination. The papers were sent out by mail to the ship and the examination, which took three days, was held under the watchful eye of the Old Man in his day-cabin. The papers would be returned to the Board of Trade for marking and months later the results would be sent to the Captain. It is hardly surprising that my marks, each year, left a lot to be desired.

The passage to Cape Town, where we were to bunker and take on stores and fresh water was, apart from little problems with the crew, more or less without incident. On arrival, the weather was fine and hot and it was the full summer holiday period with masses of people on the beaches. It was the occasion to break out my white tropical uniform. Not to wear on board of course, but to go ashore in. I was given a few hours off that afternoon and Mickey and I rushed ashore to make the most of it.

Cape Town was beautiful, full of gardens and bright tropical flowers. Hanging over the town was Table Mountain, a magnificent backdrop to the white and gaily painted buildings and houses. It was magical after years of having lived in war-torn London beneath grey skies surrounded by dirt, grime and smog in a climate of austerity and shortage.

A huge liner lay in port not far from where we were berthed. Her hull was painted in a strange †lavender-pink colour and her decks were packed with passengers. And the girls - well, this was surely heaven! The dream lasted but a short while and within a few hours we were at sea again heading for South Australia, with my white uniform back in the cupboard.

As we headed south on what I was to learn was a great-circle route (a line which follows the curvature of the globe), the weather deteriorated and it grew colder as huge seas piled up and washed over us. I must admit that there were times when I was apprehensive, if not truly frightened, as I looked out of the wheel-house windows. It seemed as though we would never make it up out of the troughs down into which we had slid. Shadowed by giant albatross, we made our way south of the 45th parallel slowly inching our way across the southern Indian Ocean.

Down in that inhospitable part of the world, it was Christmas; my first away from home. Not much in the way of gaily wrapped parcels but, at least, bravely coloured paper chains were strung up in the dining-saloon to give it a festive look. There was a Christmas spirit about with a promise of pudding and turkey in the air, although I did wonder how our Nigerian cook would handle it. As it happened, I was not able, that year, to make a comparison between a Nigerian made pudding and that made by my mother.

Christmas day dawned in the same way as any other, with my climbing up to the bridge in the dark to stand my watch with William at four o'clock in the morning. The weather was bad with huge rolling seas and we were all alone in a wide expanse of ocean with nothing but the Antarctic to the South. Several albatross kept us company: magnificent birds swooping effortless above the sea.

At eight, I had breakfast in the dining-saloon and retired to my cabin. No work on deck that day, I changed into my best uniform and started to write a letter home. Half way through the morning, Mickey knocked on my door and told me that I was required by the Old Man in the smoke-room.

The smoke-room was pleasantly panelled in polished mahogany with reproductions of paintings of London by Canaletto. The settees and armchairs were covered in green leather giving the place the look of a gentleman's London club. A number of coffee tables were bolted to the deck in front of the settees. Needless to say, other than for high days and holidays, the chief steward kept the place locked up (this was really unnecessary on my first voyage since there was no socialising between the officers on board. After having taken their meals, each would retire to his cabin or go on watch without so much as a word spoken. Not a happy ship).

Today, however, it was different. On entering, I saw that in addition to the Old Man, the chief engineer, chief officer and chief steward, in the guise of chief catering officer, were there, all drinking neat Gordon's Gin and obviously slightly the worse for wear. With exception of the chief engineer who wore his only blue serge suit with its insignia of Fremlin's Brown Ale proudly displayed, everyone wore their best uniform; an impressive display of gold braid.

By way of opening the conversation, the Old Man asked me what I thought of Welsh choirs. Up until then, my views on such things were somewhat limited but I had heard somewhere, of the eisteddfods at which Druids (?) sang. Also wasn't it true that the Rhondda Valley was famous for its choirs?

"Lovely singing", I said, hoping that this was an appropriate answer.

"Right boyo" said the "Old Man". "Now you climb up on that table". He pointed to one of the coffee tables, "and sing us a song".

Bad news, I thought to myself. Either I didn't understand what he had said or, if I had, then things were going to get tricky. Either way, I was in trouble. Other than for the sound of clattering of plates and cutlery coming from the dining-saloon, a silence fell as everyone's attention was focused upon me.

"Up on the table boyo!" the "Old Man" ordered. Having no alternative, I managed to hoist myself up onto the table but had great difficulty in maintaining my balance because of the swooping movement of the ship as she rolled and pitched.

"Now, sing us a song".

"Sir", I said, "I don't know any songs". Faced with my negative performance, the Old Man was getting visibly irritated "I didn't ask you if you knew any songs, I simply told you to sing a song".

There was no answer that I could think of at that moment and I remained mute, trying to keep myself from falling off the table. I remember thinking that it would be nice if, at that moment, we could hit an iceberg and sink like the "Titanic". It was about the only thing that could resolve my problem.

Having stood there, numb with embarrassment for a few moments, the "Old Man" told me to get down off the table and go to my cabin. I was to get undressed, get into my bunk and stay there until it was time to get up for me to go on watch at 4 o'clock. I was to have no lunch or tea (dinner) and he would send the third officer to check that I had carried out his orders.

So ended my first Christmas as sea. To this day, I have never understood why a grown man, old enough to be my father who had, I presume experienced all sorts of fear and hardship during the war, should do this to a sixteen year old lad.

The crossing from South Africa to Adelaide took 28 days without sight of land. By the time we arrived at Adelaide, we had run out of fresh food and water. Back to corned beef and would you believe, hardtack biscuits. The very same that one could expect to eat on board a clipper rounding Cape Horn at the end of the nineteenth century. These would be soaked in a little water to soften them up and made into a sort of porridge; salt, condensed milk or sugar to taste.

Chapter 19

That first night, after docking, most of the crew went "on the piss" for lack of a better expression. This must have been part of a regular feature in Adelaide for the padre of the Flying Angel Missions to Seamen came on board and took me ashore to the mission outside the docks where I was offered lemonade, buns and a game of darts. My first steps ashore in Australia! He need not have worried too much about me for I was beginning to "shape up" a bit and develop a sense of survival.

The following morning became the first of a long association with "Chippy" the ship's carpenter. William informed me that henceforth, whilst on the Australian coast, I would assist the carpenter. This was good news. Although I had hardly exchanged two words with him during the voyage from London, Chippy had seemed to me to be an educated person with a fine manner. He was known to the sailors as Baron Windlass because he operated this piece of machinery and also because of his aloof personality.

In a sense, we were two of a kind and it wasn't long before I was being known as Freddy, Viscount Fo'clehead. This was an illusion to the fact that Chippy's workshop lay beneath the fo'c'le head and our duty consisted of the maintenance of the ship's hatch-boards, cargo-battens, limber-boards down in the bilges, and the freshwater tanks. The latter had to be periodically cleaned and coated internally with a cement-wash. Not amusing work, particularly in the tropics.

I was never very good at carpentry but thanks to "Chippy" that voyage, I learnt a great deal on the technical side. Also, a lot about the cinema and films in general of which he was a great fan!

I was to be "borrowed" occasionally from Chippy to clean out the bilges and other such jobs that the sailors might have required additional pay. Even so, my working hours on the Australian coast, although long, were a lot easier than those spent at sea.

That second day in Adelaide was interesting. During the voyage Mickey had told me that William had been infuriated by the fact that his neighbour, the *Admiral*, kept him awake part of the night with his accordion and Estonian folk songs. He had complained bitterly several times, but the *Admiral*, continued to ignore him. By the time we reached Adelaide, there existed a climate of hate between the two.

On the afternoon following our arrival, William, very much the worse for wear after a night's boozing, had collapsed unconscious onto his bunk. The fact that he was unconscious probably saved his life. Having no specific duties, the *Admiral*, had once again locked himself in his room; this time with a bottle of vodka which he had probably smuggled on board the night before.

I happened to be walking down the weather-deck alleyway from N.2 hatch towards N.3 when, having arrived almost outside the *Admiral,'s* open port hole, I heard a crash and a terrible scream. I rushed into the accommodation and found the chief officer's door wide open. Running into his room, I found the *Admiral*, trying desperately to dislodge a fire-axe which was embedded in the mahogany panelling a few inches above William's face. It seems that the *Admiral*, had tried to decapitate him but that the swing of the axe had been a little too energetic. The result was that the axe head was well and truly embedded in the panelling. Failing to dislodge the axe, the *Admiral*, spitting fury, was trying to strangle William with his bare hands. I tried to pull the *Admiral* off but he was far too strong for me. I was rewarded for my efforts with a punch in the face. By this time, the commotion we were making had woken up the chief steward from this siesta who came lumbering in. Our weightlifting champion threw himself at the *Admiral*, who collapsed onto the deck beneath the enormous weight of the onslaught. I shouted to the Radio officer to run ashore and telephone for help. Screaming in Russian (or was it Estonian?) the *Admiral* continued his struggles to try to get to William to finish him off. By this time, we had gathered quite an audience and, with help, managed to tie up the unfortunate *Admiral*. It was clear by this time that something had gone badly wrong in his head.

The last I ever saw of him, he was trussed up in a straightjacket and was being carried ashore down the gangway lashed to a stretcher to a waiting ambulance. The padre from the Flying Angel Mission came by some time later to collect the *Admiral's* concertina and his few pathetic belongings. I often wonder what happened to the poor man.

We were now short of a Second Officer. On completion of discharge of our Adelaide cargo, which had been effected without incident so far as I can recall, the authorities produced a new Second Officer just before sailing, leaving the "Old Man" no choice in the matter. He was short, with a flowing white beard and had, some years previously apparently commanded sailing ships on the Chilean nitrate and guano run across the Pacific, but was now retired. It was said that he knew the Great Barrier Reef like the back of his hand.

Unfortunately, it was discovered that his eyesight left a lot to be desired. It didn't take much imagination, even for me at that time that left alone on the bridge to navigate among the coral islands of the Barrier Reef, we were likely to end our days like Robinson Crusoe.

From Adelaide we sailed to Melbourne and then to Sydney where the rest of the cargo from London was discharged. Thoughts of picking our way through a maze of coral islands to the north made the Captain think that it was perhaps time to check the lifeboats whilst we were at anchor in the calm waters of Sydney harbour and whilst awaiting instructions concerning a new cargo.

It was decided to launch the motor lifeboat. Although duly inscribed in the log book to the contrary, we had not, in fact, actually had any such thing as a boat drill during the outward passage from England (and Wales). I cannot say that our first attempt would have been applauded by the Board of Trade Examiner, had he been there.

With the help of a few sailors milling about, the boat was eventually freed of its rusted lashings and swung out over the side. Manually, the boat was lowered slowly to the water. It is normal for lifeboats to take on board their complement of crew and passengers from the boat-deck as shown in the film "Titanic". We were not the "Titanic" however and had our own way of doing things. The Old Man decided that I, together with William and the second engineer should climb down a rope ladder to board the board once it was floating.

As it turned out it was a very wise precaution. When the level of the boat reached about a metre from the surface of the water there was a shout from the sailor controlling the forward rope fall and the lifeboat nose-dived into the sea and hung suspended from the after fall. The oars and gear were catapulted into the water, to float away on the morning tide. The cause of this calamity was immediately apparent. The forward rope fall was too short and had at some time "lost" a length from one end. Obviously, this would never have been apparent had the *Sunbridge* not been floating high in the water and empty of cargo.

Being the youngest and presumably the most agile, I was told to swim out and recover the floating gear that lay all around. Meanwhile the after end of the boat was lowered gently without causing a tidal wave to flood the interior. Eventually William and the second engineer managed to clamber down into the boat, cast off and came to pick me up. We recovered all the gear that floated, and as it was a beautifully calm, hot day, we decided to go for a spin around the harbour, one of the most beautiful in the world. The second engineer's baby, the engine, had been overhauled by him and surprised me by working without a hitch. Just as well. I soon realised we were leaking like a sieve and very quickly we settled deep into the water Things then became a bit desperate. We headed back to the ship as quickly as possible and I baled for all I was worth trying to keep the level of water from reaching the engine. We only just made it back under oars, the water having eventually flooded over the engine.

By this time, the shortened fall had been spliced with a new length of rope and we were just able to make fast before the boat sank. It was eventually emptied and hauled back up on board where inspection showed that a number of planks had opened up. We had no oakum with which to caulk the boat but the chief steward produced a number of large rolls of cotton-wool from "his" store. This, mixed with a white lead paste from the paint locker was hammered into the seams between the planks. A coat of white paint was duly applied by me and the boat was declared to be as good as new (throughout the four years I was to remain on board, the boat was never again put into the water, although the engine was put back into working condition by the second engineer, presumably to the entire satisfaction of the Board of Trade examiner who would, each year, examine our life saving equipment).

During our stay in Sydney, I witnessed something which was to mark me for life. Whilst alongside discharging, our berth was next to that of the passenger terminal. Adjacent to this was a vast wired-in open space or compound. It was not long before I found out what this was for. It was to contain many hundreds of displaced persons being disembarked from aged pre-war P & O liners such as the ss *Mooltan* (these were referred to as the Black Ships, whose hulls and funnels were black and whose superstructures were painted in a dirty yellow colour). They had been requisitioned to carry people from various internment and concentration camps in Central Europe. Very similar to the rush of Irish immigrants into the United States one hundred years ago.

Chapter 20

After two days at anchor in Sydney harbour, we received instructions to proceed to Brisbane to load bagged raw sugar. It was now the end of March and I had been away from home for five months.

Brisbane came and went without any lasting recollection. Our "Ancient Mariner", the Second Officer, did not quite fit in and was replaced by a much younger man whose past wasn't too clear. I think that some time previously he had jumped ship, had become disenchanted with life in Australia and wanted to return to England. He had a bit of a drink problem and his hands shook badly. Nevertheless he seemed to be a good navigating officer at sea. In port, well, that was another problem that was, in the end, to kill him. Saying that he had been a paratrooper, he jumped from the bridge onto the quayside - a drop equivalent to throwing oneself out of a third floor window.

From Brisbane we sailed north to Urangan to load a further quantity of raw-sugar in bags. Urangan was a "T" shaped jetty jutting out from a superb sandy beach. There was absolutely nothing else there but a small sailing club and a few houses. The nearest town, Maryborough, lay inland to the south some twenty miles away by road. The jetty formed the terminus of a rail connection where wagons loaded with sugar at the mill arrived for discharge.

I imagine that the local population of Maryborough had little in the way of entertainment and the occasional arrival of a ship at Urangan provided an excuse for an outing. Although by no means did we resemble the "Queen Mary", we attracted hundreds of visitors over the weekend. We were literally overrun. The weather was magnificent and hot and the adjacent beach was crowded.

We stayed there for a whole week and of course with all the girls around, it were inevitable that I should fall in love! Her name was Pat. She was seventeen, she was pretty with short brown curly hair and blue eyes, and had lovely long legs shown off to the best advantage beneath a flimsy miniskirt; totally enchanting. She, like many others, had come on board to look around - for her, a first visit to a ship. I had spotted her in the midst of the crowd of visitors and had proposed to give her a private guided tour of the bridge (whose brass gleamed in the afternoon sunlight and of which I was justly proud!). Fortunately, for the occasion, I was not in my dungarees but wore my whites with epaulettes. It was a Saturday afternoon; no work on deck for me that day. Very keen, I showed her the workings of the bridge controls and instruments (not a great deal in those days) and my refuge, the monkey-island. After a tour of the ship and engine-room came a tour of my cabin - fortunately the cooks had gone ashore. Not a much there, but it was mine. It was love at first sight!

Afterwards we went for a long walk along the beach and swam in the warm clear water until sunset (Pat's friend, who was older and possessed a small car had disappeared with our radio officer). Both girls decided to return on the following day with picnics and we spent the whole day just laying about on the beach and getting sunburnt. Marvellous after all that which had gone on during the voyage.

Time passed too quickly, I knew that my love-life with Pat was pretty precarious. The chances of ever seeing Pat again and returning to Urangan were pretty slim. Nevertheless, one could always hope that something would turn up. On the evening before we sailed, we promised to write to each other. At least that was something.

We sailed for Mackay, a small town in Queensland.

The first Sunday in Mackay, William decided to invite on board three "nurses from the local hospital". Being port side to the quay, he thought it a good idea to impress the ladies with a bit of seamanship by lowering the starboard lifeboat into the water and going for a bit of a sail around the harbour. Unlike the port side boat, this one did not have an engine. It was decided that I, together with the Second Officer as crew, should accompany him and his guests.

Looking back, I now have a serious doubt about the profession of these ladies. By the time they had boarded the lifeboat they were rather the worse for wear with gin provided by William. This time there were no mishaps in lowering the boat and once in the water, we cast off in fair seamanship manner, rigged up the mast and set sail.

Unfortunately with all the effort of getting the mast up and sorting out the rigging, we failed to notice that the boat was rapidly filling up with water. Accompanied by screams of hysterical laughter from the ladies, we turned about and frantically rowed our way back to the ship. By the time we got back, we were sinking. The sight of our lady guests, soaking wet in their Sunday best frocks, climbing up a rope ladder to get back on board was something that I'll never forget. No doubt William revived them after their ordeal at sea with a large gin and tonic.

I had, once again, recourse to using the chief steward's rolls of cotton wool. To this day, I am not sure if cotton wool works in caulking boats but luckily we were never to have the occasion again to test the floatability of either the port or the starboard boat.

Chapter 21

Fully loaded with a cargo of sugar in bags, we sailed from Mackay in April 1951 for Vancouver by way of Honolulu for bunkers. I saw nothing of Honolulu that voyage since we were there for only four hours but from what I saw of it, it reminded me a little of Cape Town. A place to come back to! We arrived in Vancouver, just one month after having left the Australian coast.

I had not really been aware that on my mother's side we had remote cousins living in Vancouver. My mother, however, had written to tell them of my impending arrival.

On the quayside, awaiting our arrival therefore was Edward Lambert. Edward, or "Mate" as he was known, ran an insurance office and his wife, Juliet, owned a very smart boutique in Vancouver, selling women's fashions. They had two daughters, Claudette the elder, who was about eighteen and Pat who was much younger, about six. Claudette had just started her medical studies at a teaching hospital in Vancouver.

It's sad, but being young at the time and having little inclination toward the study of family trees, I never asked the Canadian Lamberts about their ancestors and how they had arrived, in Canada. Originally from Paris, during the French Revolution, they had fled France, gone to London and finally, had settled in British Colombia. I am ashamed to say that after a second visit to Vancouver in 1952, we lost sight of each other.

On that first visit to Canada, they persuaded the "Old Man" to give me some time off and, with great kindness, took me around and showed me part of this beautiful country.

All too soon we completed discharge and sailed for two small timber ports in the United States. Raymond and Grays Harbour, Washington. There we commenced to load a cargo of American sawn timber.

In Raymond, as the ship was more or less empty, it was decided that the draft marks, showing the depth of the vessel in the water, should be repainted since they had become barnacle encrusted during the voyage and were no longer readable.

My prowess at handling a lifeboat in Australia had not gone unnoticed! I was ordered to carry out this operation from one the "jolly boats". These were small open boats carried, in addition to the lifeboats, for emergency purposes. The oars and gear were removed and replaced with pots of black and white paint and appropriate brushes. I was given two seamen to moor the boat aft and I secured it under the overhanging stern with lines leading down from the weather deck. This would enable me to reach and scrape off the seaweed and growth from the drafts marks and repaint them.

By the time I had launched the boat, hauled it aft under the counter stern and secured it so that it was held tightly against the hull, it was mid-afternoon. The weather at that stage of the operation was not brilliant with a light wind blowing and an ebbing tide causing the boat to rock from side to side, not ideal for sign-painting but still alright for scraping off barnacles. Whilst I was busy at this, I began to realise that the sea was getting rougher and that the gunwale of the boat was slamming up against the hull in such a way that I could hardly keep my balance. I decided that the weather no longer permitted me to continue and that I should return the boat to the falls and have it hoisted it up clear of the water.

Shouting up to the two seamen on deck to release the boat and haul me round, I received no answer; they had gone for a cup of tea. By the time they returned a quarter of an hour later, the wind had increased and the sea had risen considerably, smashing the boat violently up under the counter stern. I was furious and not a little frightened at being left alone. Not only that, but the open pots of black and white paint which I had neglected to wedge up and secure, had tipped over with the violent motion of the boat and spilt paint all over the bottom boards.

Gesticulating, shouting and very angry, I ordered them to release the boat from its position under the overhanging stern and pull me clear. They just stood there, looking down at me with grins on their faces and then disappeared.

Dusk was falling and it was getting cold. A light drizzle was beginning to thoroughly dampen my spirit. After ten minutes or so, they returned and without so much as a sign, they untied the lines holding the boat, then threw them down at me and walked away. Thus released, the boat swung clear of the stern of the ship and moved away at a smart pace with the tide, towards the open sea.

I stood there, wedged in, trying to keep my balance, waving and shouting and trying to get the attention of someone on board. There was no one on deck. Without oars or rudder I was powerless to do anything. As the *Sunbridge* receded into the distance and the misty rain began to seep into my clothes, I had no alternative but to settle myself down and wait for someone to rescue me. The boat had turned broadside to the waves and was rolling unchecked on her beam-ends. I managed to crawl to a place on the bottom boards beneath one of the thwarts away from the spilt paint and crouched there miserably, getting colder and colder as time went by.

Darkness fell and the coastline faded away leaving me adrift in the Pacific Ocean with no food, no water and, most important, no light. After a couple of hours of trying to prevent myself from being catapulted out, I must have been too exhausted to combat the cold and fell asleep.

I was told later that it was around midnight that the US Coast Guard cutter found me and towed me back to the ship. Unable to climb back up the rope ladder to board the ship, the Coast Guards took me round to the quay and helped me aboard by way of the gangway. The boat was left, tied up to the quay, ahead of the ship.

Feeling decidedly the worse for wear the following morning, I was told that the "Old Man" wanted to see me. As he had not formed part of the reception committee the night before, I rather expected that he would at least be glad to see that I was still alive. I could not have been more wrong. The "Old Man" was hopping mad. He had been presented with a bill for my rescue from the US Coast Guard which the company & Owners would have to pay. All this he told me, because of my incredible stupidity; a full report of my ineptitude would be sent to London.

I felt that my case would not best be served if I tried to explain that it had not really been my fault and that the two seamen delegated to help me had been responsible. I decided to say nothing but would try and settle the score with the two men later.

As punishment, the "Old Man" ordered me to remain on board and cancelled permission to go ashore until our return to England.

In defiance of orders, I sneaked ashore on a couple of nights with Chippy, Baron Windless, went to the cinema and saw "Apache Drums" and "The Bride Wore Spurs".

We finally sailed for home, or at least, Southampton, at the end of June 1951. After a last call on the Pacific Coast of the United States at San Diego to bunker, we headed for home via the Panama Canal. The passage to Southampton where we arrived on the 3rd August 1951 was without incident.

In fact, I was never able to get my own back against the two men who had set me adrift; they were bigger than me and anyway, I had no allies amongst the seamen.

Something which I will never forget; on the morning before we arrived at Southampton, I was on watch with William as usual when, out of the early morning mist, loomed the "Queen Elisabeth". She passed us at close quarters and as I gazed in wonder at this magnificent, exceptional sight from my old tramp steamer, wondering what life on board such a vessel could be like.

So ended my first trip on the *Sunbridge*. I had made it back, perhaps a little wiser in the ways of men, but by no means fireproof. Anyway, I was now pretty good at washing out my dungarees and ironing shirts. My maths, physics and navigation had still not improved however but at least I was now handy with a scrubbing brush and paint scraper.

Following our arrival in Southampton, I was sent home on leave for ten days. It was almost ten months since I had last seen my parents.

Although somewhat at a loss to know what to do with my time since I was not called upon to scrub floors of chip rust with a hammer, my leave at home passed quickly and once again, I found myself back on the Sunbridge in Southampton. This time, I had a little time to look around and saw a profusion of big liners which seemed to me to be part of another world. I saw for a second time those Union-Castle liners with their pink hulls which I had seen previously in Cape Town. From my humble position aboard a tramp ship they represented another world, totally foreign to mine; to achieve this universe seemed to me to be utterly beyond my reach.

Chapter 22

I wasn't allowed to look around for long. My next flight into the unknown was beginning. We sailed in ballast with a scratch crew from Southampton on the 16th August 1951 bound for Liverpool where we entered drydock. Same sordid performance as before in Newport, but fortunately for three days only.

Once out of dock we commenced to load a full cargo of general merchandise for Australia, but for two ports only, Freemantle and Adelaide. A fresh crew of seamen from South Wales arrived. The last one was bad enough, but this one showed itself to be particularly nasty.

It was inevitable that after nearly a year on board the *Sunbridge* I knew my way about and to a certain extent, had "shaped-up". I was not going to let this crew of Welshmen walk all over me. This, unfortunately was easier said than done, and I had not really yet learnt that in certain conditions, discretion is the better part of valour.

I was in trouble even before we had left the English Channel. My brilliance at scraping and chipping rust, scrubbing decks, shovelling garbage and other such uplifting works had led the "Old Man" to economise on crew expenses by not taking on the customary deck-boy. It seemed that I could adequately fill this position in addition to my studies and normal duties on the four to eight watch. Proficient on the helm, this in itself economised on one able-seaman, and I envisaged that in another year or so I might find myself equal to three or four able-seaman plus a deck-boy thrown in for good measure. I would thus make a substantial contribution to the profit of the voyage and to the wealth of the ship-owner.

I mention this because the absence of a deck-boy meant that I now had to carry the seamen's breakfast from the galley to the crew accommodation, aft, each morning at six-thirty. In bad weather, this was a rough and wet passage requiring the skill of a five-star hotel room-service waiter in gum boots and southwester. I cheered myself up with the thought that all else having failed, I could always get a job as a first-class waiter on the "Queen Elisabeth".

The punctuality of this operation relied on my being relieved from the helm by my co-watch keeper able seaman. This meant that for twenty minutes or so, he would have to take over the wheel as I went about my catering duties. This, needless to say, he objected to. He manifested his discontent by often arriving on the bridge, five or even ten minutes late.

My lateness on arrival in the galley infuriated the Nigerian cook who "had better things to do with his time than keep the crew breakfast hot". In fact, much of the time the goo that passed for porridge was already cold and the passage across the after weather-deck at the mercy of seas breaking over it, normally fixed it altogether. The mess of so called scrambled eggs had hardened into lumps. By and large, the breakfasts, by the time they arrived in the crew mess-room, were not quite as appetising as one could have wished. The mood of the seamen as I arrived, ten or fifteen minutes late, with their congealed meal left a lot to be desired. Unfortunately on some occasions this resulted in my being knocked around and cuffed about the ears.

Now it transpired that amongst the deck crew was a man from some small valley or other in South Wales who went under the name of Jones. He was not like the others, to say the least. Not willing to share a cabin with three others he had taken his mattress and bedding and made himself a "home" amongst the mooring ropes and rats in the lazaret or what had once been the ammunition locker, right aft, over the rudder.

Since he neither washed nor shaved, the absence of conveniences did not seem to bother him. Armed at all times with a long, wicked looking knife, the crew was afraid of him, left him strictly alone. His strange behaviour left little doubt that he was not only mentally deranged, but also, dangerous. It's unlikely in this day and age that such a person would be permitted to walk the streets, but there he was, on the *Sunbridge*, and entirely free.

Even William who had survived a hate crazed assault by an Estonian admiral, kept well clear of him. Jones did not take his meals with the others but only took what he wanted from the aluminium dishes and simply went to find a sheltered spot on deck to eat.

I had seen him watching me from the corner of his eye when I received the none too gentle treatment from the others at breakfast time, but like them, I thought that there was something sinister about him and kept well clear.

One morning, about one week after departure from Liverpool, my relief on the wheel had been particularly slow in taking my place and it was nearly seven o'clock, time to start work for the deck hands, before I could collect the breakfasts from the galley. I had already had a row with the cook and was in no mood to be messed about but I knew that I was heading for trouble in the crew mess-room. To my utter surprise, as I arrived at the entrance of the crew accommodation, Jones stood there and signed me to give him the aluminium kits that contained the breakfasts. With these in his hands he turned and went down the stairs to the crew mess. I stood there, waiting for the outburst that would surely came from the seamen. There was not a sound and thereafter, for most of the voyage to Freemantle, he waited for me at the entrance of the crew accommodation and took the breakfasts down to the crew himself. From then on my relief on the helm was never so much as minute late.

I expected retribution around each corner but none came. Instead, when working on deck alongside the crew during the day. I found that Jones had managed to get the same job as me and we worked together, side by side. Whilst I would talk to him and chatter on about my life, he would never reply or say a word about himself. He remained mute, but I nevertheless had the distinct impression that he appreciated my company.

As days passed, he would always be there next to me, my protector, my shadow. The crew, as though I was a leper, kept away from me as much as possible and life for me returned to normal. I even had no further aggravation from the cook, except, of course on the matter of cleaning the alleyway.

Instead to going around the Cape of Good Hope as we had done on the last voyage, we made our way to Australia by way of the Suez Canal and down the Red Sea to Aden where we bunkered. From there, we headed down through the Indian Ocean. As we reached the southern latitudes, the weather worsened and it became cold as it had done on the previous trip; the latitudes of the albatross and empty seas.

One afternoon, a few days before we were due to arrive at Freemantle, Western Australia, I was working on deck alongside my friend and protector, Jones. A rough sea was running and the vessel was rolling and pitching heavily. We were engaged in the filthy job of oiling the steel deck on the starboard side of the weather deck at N.3 hatch, between the bridge and the engineer's accommodation. We shared a big bucket of oil filled with a mixture of tar and fish oil, and, on our hands and knees, we applied this with our bare hands to the deck with a wad of cotton-waste.

As usual, we were working alone. Apparently deep in thought and, of course, saying nothing as usual, Jones got to his feet abruptly, walked to the side of the ship and without a backward glance, climbed up onto the rails and threw himself into the sea.

I rushed up onto the bridge and gave the alarm but was shocked to see that no one cared. The noise I was creating roused the Old Man who ordered the ship to turn about to search the area. Much too late, we retraced our route for a few minutes but never saw trace of him. Although he was utterly strange, I felt a strange sympathy for him and was deeply saddened by his action. I felt that if only I had been able to communicate properly with him I might have been able to prevent this tragedy.

On arrival at Freemantle, not so much as a question was raised on his disappearance. I suppose the "Old Man" must have been questioned by the authorities but no one came and asked me what had happened. I had been, after all, the last one to see him alive.

We stayed in Freemantle for a couple of weeks discharging our cargo and then sailed for Adelaide, a trip of seven days. There, we duly completed the discharge in the space of three weeks. I had hoped that we might receive instructions to load again a cargo of sugar in Queensland but this was not to be. Pat was in Maryborough, nearly two thousand miles away from Adelaide. Not an easily attempted journey for an impoverished cadet officer earning seventy-five pounds a year! The good news for me however was that we were to return to Vancouver.

We departed from Adelaide during the first week of December 1951 in ballast, there being no cargo available at that time for us to take to Canada. We reached Honolulu on Christmas day. This time, there was no time for the singing of songs, Welsh, Carols, or otherwise. I worked on deck, took my Christmas "dinner" in the pantry, which was an improvement on having to sit in the dining saloon with the others and tried to ignore the fact that it was Christmas. Certainly, the surroundings helped. No snow here: white, sandy beaches, sparkling turquoise sea, palm trees, luxuriant vegetation and bright green forest covered mountains, all beneath a warm, clear blue sky.

After lunch I changed into my white tropical uniform, went ashore on my own and joined the throngs of brightly clothed Americans in town. I strolled along Waikiki Beach, watching the surfers, ogled the girls and because of my uniform, was invited by kind strangers interested by my "cute accent" to partake of my first ever banana-split. An enormous affair, overflowing with chocolate, nuts, chantilly cream and topped overall with real orchids - quite an improvement on cook's soggy Christmas pud. All too soon, however, the dream was over. I returned to the ship in Pearl Harbour and a few hours later, we resumed our voyage to Vancouver.

We arrived there some time during the first week in January 1952. It was dark, cold and wet but once again, the warm hearted, kind Lamberts went out of their way to entertain and look after me. We stayed in Vancouver only a few days, loading a cargo of Canadian softwood. On parting from the Lamberts I hoped that we should see each other in the future, but sadly, this was not to be and I never saw them again. Letters we subsequently exchanged have been lost and I now have no trace of them, which is sad.

Chapter 23

Our sawn timber cargo was destined for a town called Tarakan which is in Borneo. So, once again we trundled across the Pacific Ocean, with a brief call at Honolulu. No time, on this occasion to sample another king-sized banana split.

Nearly two weeks after having left Honolulu, west bound, on the 6th February 1952, we received the news that King George VI had died; it was just after lunch. The Old Man sent for me and told that as a mark of respect I was to change into my best white uniform, and to hoist our ensign aft on the poop deck (we had no gaff from which to fly it), then to bring it down slowly to half-mast in proper fashion as a sign of mourning. I was then to stand there until I received orders to take down the flag and return to the bridge (at sea, on ocean passages, clear of land, it was not the custom to fly an ensign).

Now, whilst it was not cold, it was blowing a gale and we were shipping seas overall. The vessel was pitching and rolling to such an extent that although loaded to our marks, the propeller was racing half out of the water part of the time as we crested a wave. By the time I reached the poop, I was soaked and as we fell into a trough, my lunch, such as it was in storm conditions, was trying to find its way out of my throat. Coming out of the trough was like being in an express lift going up with one's legs being forced up through one's skull. With some difficulty, I clipped on the ensign and raised it to the staff-head where it stood out like a board trying to take me overboard. Finally, I managed to master it and dragged it down to half mast in the prescribed manner and secured it. For some reason, I imagined that I had performed well. Homage had been observed and after all, the flag had not been ripped out of my hands to be lost to the waves. I waited expectantly to receive a sign from the bridge to return. It seemed however, that the poor George VI, for whom I had much admiration, must have been revered by the Old Man to the point of obsession, for no such sign arrived. I was left out in the wet, soaked through, holding on to the taffrail for dear life, for over three hours until it was time for me to go back on watch at four o'clock. By that time, the ensign had been shredded and less than half of it remained, just part of the union flag, half surrounded by strips of red cloth. I still wonder if it had been intentional or simply a matter of having forgotten me out there in stormy conditions. In any event it was all part of a process of being "shaped up"!

On our way to Borneo, during our stop over in Honolulu, the Old Man had received from the Board of Trade in Cardiff, the first of my yearly examination papers. After leaving Honolulu therefore, I was informed that I was to present myself to the captain in his day-room where I would sit my examination; this was to last three days.

Now, I had done my best to work at my maths, physics, navigation and seamanship during my free time, but in all fairness, I'd had little of this during the past year and could hardly say that I was well prepared for the coming exam! Navigation and seamanship were all right, and after all, had I not "shaped up". But my maths and physics were still a disaster area.

During those three days the Old Man took his role of supervisor very seriously and watched me like a hawk - no way of cheating. My algebraic equations still did not want to equal out but somehow I managed to complete the papers set before me in the required time. I imagined that the results would not be much to write home about.

Months later, when the results were sent out by the Board of Trade to the Old Man, I was hauled over the coals and told once again, that I had better "shape up". Nothing changed! (Before I was eventually to leave the *Sunbridge* I underwent two further examinations each more advanced and difficult than the previous. Each time, since my condition remained unchanged, the results were poor, followed months later by a vicious tongue lashing about my ineptitude from the captain. All this, I suppose, to make sure that I did not get ideas above my station.

Following our discharge of the timber in Borneo, we proceeded to Colombo where, of all things, we dry-docked. If the sanitary conditions in Newport and Liverpool were bad, those of Colombo were unspeakable. Fortunately we were not there for more than a few days before going on in ballast to Calcutta where we arrived some time in mid -April 1952. We were to load coal in bulk. One of the most trying experiences of my life.

Calcutta lies on the Hooghly river, some hundred and twenty miles upstream on the Ganges Delta. On picking up the pilot who was to guide us up river to Calcutta, I was amazed to see that this sahib Englishman in pristine white naval uniform sporting an impressive amount of gold braid, was accompanied by his Indian servant complete with a massive trunk and, would you believe it, a huge brass telescope.

The filth, the heat, the flies and everything covered in coal-dust. The coal was grabbed out of rail wagons and dropped from a great height into our holds. I was sent spitting and coughing around the decks with my faithful shovel and a broom. All day, every day, beneath a smog filled sky through which the sun, a red orb in the dust, glared down vengefully, I swept up the masses of coal which had showered down onto the decks. I became blacker than the Nigger Minstrels and resembled the miners coming up out of their pits in the Rhondda Valley in South Wales. The difference was that I was not singing nor swigging Burton's Fine Ale. This hellish existence lasted a little over two weeks.

On the brighter side, the Padre of the Flying Angel Missions to Seamen discovered my presence on board and decided that I needed rescuing. Every evening, he came on board and took me ashore. He introduced me to the Swimming Club of Calcutta. This was a fully fledged British Raj institution open only to white sahibs of course; memsahibs too, I supposed.

I was asked to join water-polo team in their practice matches. This, to my mind, was only just preferable to shovelling coal, for I was a poor swimmer - and still am. Each night's sporting activities resulted in my being more or less drowned. Good clean fun I suppose. What struck me most was that on getting out of the pool and going to the changing room after the practice match, Indian servants awaited us, removed our trunks and dried us with huge white fluffy bath towels. I am afraid that I could not quite get to grips with this and refused to allow "my" servant to pull down my trunks and much less let him wipe me down. I was not, after all, incapable of looking after myself. This was not looked upon with much favour by my team -mates; sahibs were sahibs and Indians were Indians, after all. No wonder we lost our Empire.

What I saw of Calcutta that trip left me saddened with an indelible memory of mass poverty, filth, death and disease.

In contrast, standing white and clean, the pillared entrances of the clubs and mansions of the sahibs stood like jewels in a mouth of rotting teeth.

Chapter 24

I left Calcutta without regret. I put away my shovel and returned to the daily uplifting routine of chipping rust away from our poor corroded decks which were getting thinner and thinner as time passed. Our new destination was Nagasaki in Japan, via Singapore, for bunkers, where we were to discharge our coal. En route to Singapore, I developed a raging toothache and on arrival was taken ashore to a local Chinese dentist who pulled out two of my back teeth. I suppose they were the right ones, for after that I had no more trouble. The problem was that I think only one needed attention. Perhaps the dentist was paid according to the number of teeth he pulled. After my ordeal, I went to Raffles Hotel for a drink to cheer myself up. Another world!

We continued our journey to Japan and discharged our cargo there without mishap within a couple of weeks. It was then getting on for the end of May.

Of Japan, I have no clear recollection probably because I was not allowed ashore. We were berthed alongside a heavy industrial plant, some distance away from town. I didn't see anything of Nagasaki, or at least, what was left of the ruins of the city after having been destroyed by an atom bomb which had killed eighty thousand persons.

It was back to my shovel as we completed discharge. I hoped never ever again to be involved in handling coal.

From Nagasaki, we sailed in ballast for Red China. I never understood how it was that with a murderous war raging at that time in Korea between the armies of North Korea and China on one hand and the United States and the United Kingdom on the other, we should be steaming with all insouciance into what was supposed to be enemy territory. Not only that, but we were to load a strategic cargo of iron-ore and carry it to another hard-line communist country, Romania.

On arrival at Tsingtao, a contingent of heavily armed Chinese garlic chewing soldiers came on board and ransacked all the cabins in search of opium or heaven knows what.

Everything I possessed was tipped out onto the deck of my cabin in a heap, books, and clothes personal items. Angrily, I dared to protest against this. For my pains I received a vicious prod with a bayonet accompanied by a lot of incomprehensible shouting. Shortly after this, the entire crew including the "Old Man" was lined up on the hatchway of N.2 hold and received a massive injection in the arm "to protect us against the American plague bombs". Same needle for all, I had the somewhat dubious pleasure of seeing two or three of my Welsh, hard-case sailors collapse in a dead-faint at this treatment. In all fairness, I never suffered any after effects from whatever was pumped into my veins. I sometimes wonder if, in fact, I'm still protected against the bubonic plague. One never knows, it might come in useful one day.

After this, a gang of labourers came on board and rigged up a number of loudspeakers on deck. We were soon to find out what these were for. Everybody mustered on deck and counted each morning at six, followed by an hour's full blast harangue on the evils of capitalism, screamed at us by some sort of obsessed, mad political officer. We were the "spineless puppets of American imperialism", worse than nothing, and presumably in need of being "shaped up". After that, a normal day's work could start.

Loading was interminable mainly because of the lack of cargo available alongside. When the iron-ore finally arrived in wagons and trucks it was grabbed up and dumped into the holds in bulk; not quite as messy as coal but not far off. I was back to shovelling. Forbidden access ashore, my sole entertainment was the daily morning sermon, shouted and screamed at by our demented political commissar. At times I thought that at any moment we would be conscripted into the Chinese army and made to fight alongside their gallant allies, the North Koreans.

It was with a huge sense of relief that we sailed from Chinese waters at the end of the first week in June 1952. All their efforts at turning me into a right-thinking communist were in vain. I did not like their manners.

Chapter 25

One month later we arrived in Constanza on the Black sea coast of Romania. The only interesting part of the voyage was the passage through the Dardanelles, past Gallipoli and into the Sea of Marmara. I was overwhelmed at the sight, on the left bank, of hundreds of thousands of white grave stones marking the cemetery of those British and Commonwealth soldiers who had fallen, fighting the Turks, during a massive exercise in military folly during the summer of 1915.

The passage past Istanbul and through the Bosphorus was a delight to the eyes. It was full summer and beneath a clear blue sky, the crowded beaches, the palaces and magnificent villas we passed were like something out of a fairy story. Could hardly believe that the grim north China coast formed part of the same world.

Reality however, soon caught up with us again as we entered the port of Constanza. There was absolutely nothing to laugh about here either. No morning sermons but, if one could understand Romanian, one could, if so desired, listen to the loudspeakers ashore on the quayside exhorting the workers to a greater effort. Had I been able to understand, this might have been useful for me in my efforts with a shovel for I was back at it again. William was not one to vary my pleasures. The benign smile of comrade Stalin looked down upon us from everywhere where it was possible to post up a poster. The not so benign political police, with sky-blue caps, was on the quay, keeping a watchful eye out for those whose actions or thoughts did not quite follow the right line. This seemed to happen more frequently than in

China and I saw several poor wretches ashore being knocked about and marched away for having apparently deviated from the path of true thinking. Not allowed ashore, I watched this from the fragile safety of the deck, ever thankful that the local Wickford bobby did not wear a sky blue helmet.

Having received from Pat in Australia no replies to my letters during the past few months, her image had somewhat faded. It was not surprising therefore that I was now ripe for further romance.

Her name was Maria and she drove a tractor. She worked on the quayside from morning to night, pulling and pushing great wagonloads of iron ore. She was really very beautiful, about my age, with long blonde hair tied back with a red ribbon which matched nicely with the red banners which were rather prettily displayed ashore.

From what I could see, her dungarees were a lot cleaner than mine most of the time, but it was not this that attracted me. It was her shy smile directed up at me each day when no one was looking as I swept and shovelled on deck. I knew she was called Maria because every now and again, as she snatched a look in my direction and her thoughts strayed from the path of true communism, her foreman comrade -supervisor would shout her name and tell her to move it.

With no way around the soldier with his Kalashnikov on board and even less, the bluecap at the foot of the gangway, our love was doomed to fail. I could only hope, nevertheless, that the energetic way in which Maria handled her tractor would keep her out of the salt mines.

On departure from Constanza, my spirits were enlivened by the thought that at last we were homeward bound; we had received instructions to proceed in ballast to Middlesbrough.

For me, the trip homeward was spent mostly down the holds, cleaning out the bilges, sweeping up - again - and washing down the residues of coal and iron ore. When that was finished, I was set to assisting Chippy with the repairs to the wooden limber boards covering the bilges and the cargo battens which lined the ship's sides. Added to all this, of course, was my watch with William on the four to eight. I scrubbed my alleyway and delivered breakfasts, or what now passed for breakfasts, since our food supply was again down to porridge, hard-tack with weevils and corned beef stews with turnips or beetroot. In short, I was working from four in the morning to eight at night almost non-stop.

We arrived in Middlesbrough in the middle of September 1952, after having been away thirteen months. I had not set foot ashore since departure from Calcutta, more than five months previously.

Middlesbrough was steel; huge furnaces, rolling mills, piles of coal and ore, slag heaps, smoking chimneys, grit, dirt and pubs on every street corner. I had never ever seen so many pubs clustered together in one town. A place where it was said the beer was fortified and strong enough to enable the drinker to quickly forget his miserable surroundings. But at least the place was teeming with work which, perhaps, sadly, is now no longer the case.

The crew was paid-off and half the officers, including the "Old Man" went home on leave, leaving the others to look after the ship. I was told that I could go home for a week on leave. In the meantime the ship would start to load a full cargo of steel and general merchandise for discharge at a number of ports in the British West Indies.

By the time I arrived home, I had lost a bit of weight. This was somewhat dramatic since I did not weigh very much then anyway. My uniform was a couple of sizes too large. It had been purchased rather on the large size to allow for future growth. I was now not so keen to wear it as I had been previously. I do not remember a great deal about my week at home except that it took some time to adjust; it was nevertheless great to be home.

Chapter 26

By the time I returned to the ship a week later she was half loaded. A new crew had not yet been signed-on, but new Second, Third and Radio officers had arrived to replace those of the last voyage. I had had very little contact with either the Second or the Third on the previous trip and their personalities were such that I now have no recollection of whom and how they were. The same applies to the two new officers who joined us in Middlesbrough. The engineers remained unchanged but the new Radio officer was something else! Normally, I would not have had a great deal to do with the Radio officer but on this coming trip, to my dismay, this was going to change.

The "Old Man" arrived a few days before sailing with a new crew from South-Wales; a lot quieter than the previous one. I kept my head down and on the day before we completed loading, William told me that I was to have a new job; stable boy. We were to load a race - horse for discharge at Trinidad, our first port of call in the West Indies. He reminded me that I lived in the country and should know all about cows, horses and things. Now, this might well have pleased Maureen, my sister, who was a bit of a horse fan and animal lover, but for me, horses were decidedly tricky things to be observed from a long distance, or preferably, a cinema screen. I could not believe my ears; this, surely, was not a serious discussion I was having with William.

As usual, I had no one to turn to for help and I certainly possessed no literature which dealt with the subject of race horses, or cows, for that matter. On the following morning William instructed me to open up the cross-bunker - a large empty compartment which lay between number.3 hatchway and the funnel housing which had served to contain the coal bunkers. I was to empty it of accumulated rubbish, timber dunnage and ropes. It was in here that the bales of fodder, straw and the such was to be stowed. The horse box would be placed on the deck on the starboard side of number3 hatchway where a few months earlier my poor friend had jumped over side into the sea.

As I finished doing all this, the owner of the horse arrived on board, unfortunately without a horse instruction manual. A very horsey person appropriately dressed in cavalry tweed, he told me that the horse, a stallion, I forget its name, was a very valuable one. This did nothing to inspire me with confidence. He then proceeded to give me a quick ten minutes run down on how to look after, feed and water a pure-bred race horse worth thousands of pounds. This might have meant something to a stable lad with ten years experience but to me he might just as well have been speaking Chinese.

William, who had been hovering in the background, making himself inconspicuous in case he might be drawn into the conversation, suddenly came forward, slapped me on the back in fake bonhomie, as one farmer to his stable boy, and turning to the owner said cheerfully "Have no fear, this boyo is a country lad, born and bred. Been around horses and cows all his life". It was a pity, I thought, but he could have added also that my father rode to the hounds.

An impressive amount of bales of straw, hay and bags of oats and other feed duly arrived on board and was stowed in the cross-bunker. I was given a box containing what looked like scrubbing brushes, combs, buckets and sundry bits and pieces whose use I could only guess at.

The great moment arrived just before we sailed when the horse in its box was hoisted on board. The box, crudely constructed of heavy timbers, was fitted with a hinged half-height door which opened outwards. The upper part could be screened, closed by a piece of tarpaulin. The sides, internally, were padded with straw bolsters. Its width and length was barely more than that of the horse. The height of the box, fortunately, was a good deal higher than the height of the horse. Like the *Sunbridge*, the affair has seen considerable previous, rough, usage.

The owner of the animal, having seen it loaded without mishap, told me that it required no further attention that day, grabbed my hand, shook it firmly and departed down the gangway without further ado. I though that he could have at least said good bye to his horse.

During the loading operation, the canvas screen over what passed for the front door had been lashed down, presumably to prevent the horse from looking out and observing its flight over the ship's side. From the noise it was making inside, stamping and kicking, it was clear, however, that it did not take too kindly to being swung up into the air. By the time the box had been lashed down on deck by the stevedores, the operation had drawn quite a crowd from amongst the officers and crew. Everybody looked at me with great expectation. I had suddenly became the star of the show - the horse doctor.

Hiding my apprehension, I turned and drew aside the canvas curtain, much as though I was opening a punch and Judy show. There, inside, looking out at me in surprise was my new charge. He was fidgeting, disorientated, rolling his eyes and clearly unhappy with his new environment. Presumably the surrounding soot-grimed warehouses, cranes and docks together with the reeking smell of the Middlesbrough steelworks held little appeal for a pure bred racehorse from Newmarket. Before replacing the canvas cover to blot out the dismal view, I said a few appropriately soothing words in the hope that it might settle him down for his first night on board.

The following morning found us in the North Sea, heading into a stiff south-westerly wind. As I passed the box on my way to the bridge at four o'clock that morning, I paused to listen if the horse was quiet. There was not a sound and I presumed that he was sleeping. I had been told briefly by the owner, and had been surprised to learn, that horses slept standing up. What he did not tell me however was that horses suffered from sea-sickness and for the first couple of days no amount of persuasion on my part could get him to eat. He just stood there, facing out across N.3 hatchway and the blue rolling sea, with his eyes closed the very picture of dejection. In a way, this was good for me since I was able to approach him gradually without fear of being trampled to death and let him get to know me. Within a couple of days after having left Middlesbrough, we grew quite confident with each other and I was able to establish a daily routine of feeding and mucking-out worthy of the most experienced of lads. By the time we reached Trinidad a couple of weeks later, we were inseparable and the very best of friends.

I had been led to understand vaguely that at the successful completion of the voyage I should receive a reward for my labours in the form of cash from the new owner of the horse. I must admit to being sad at the sight of my friend the horse being hoisted into the air and disappearing over the side to waiting road transport, but was cheered up somewhat with the thought of a little cash coming my way. William beat me to it. As soon as he stepped on board and had inspected the horse whose coat gleamed with good health after I'd had a real go at it, the new owner was dragged into William's cabin, where, (I learnt later from Mickey who "just happened to be passing by") that a nice big brown envelope changed hands. I was never introduced to the new owner nor, in fact, did I ever see one penny of what may have been in the said brown envelope.

So much for wishful thinking. My star had set, and it was back to normal, although I did manage to obtain some advantages in the end. Because of my horse duties, I had been unable to handle the crew breakfasts and other arrangements had had to be made. After the horse had gone, I refused to return to this. It was my first act of revolt. Surprised by my violent reaction I was never again ordered to perform my job as a waiter. Anyway, I had been sufficiently "shaped up" I thought, and it was time that I should start to look after myself a bit more.

Chapter 27

The relative peace that I had enjoyed up to Trinidad on account of my special farming activities was to pass very quickly after the departure of the horse. A new problem arose from a totally unexpected quarter; the Radio officer. A small, mean, man of indeterminate age, his duties at sea had kept him more of less out of sight in his radio-room. On arrival in Trinidad, he had time on his hands and this time was to be put to a good purpose namely, the serious business of saving my soul.

Our Radio officer was a member of one of these no-nonsense religions, the Peculiar People, or Seventh Day Adventists or something like that. When he first started to lecture me, I had very foolishly told him that I was not interested in his religious leanings and that anyway I was a Roman Catholic. I might just as well have told him that I was the Devil in person.

No matter what I was doing or where I was, he would turn up and start preaching at me much along the same lines as the early pastors had done with their flocks promising them certain fire and brimstone if they did not stop their fornication and drinking.

Now, I can say in all honesty that I'd had little first-hand knowledge of such things and did not really care about what Daniel had done in the lion's den (I had previously witnessed only one sermon which had really stood out in my mind. I had felt partly involved but only because I knew some of the boys who had climbed the vicarage fence and stolen apples from the priest's garden. That Sunday morning following this dire deed, the congregation was verbally chastised by our valiant priest who terminated his sermon by shouting at us that Wickford was the "cesspool of Essex". Great sermon but this did not endear him to his parishioners).

The daily harassment of being preached at may not sound particularly important but for me, unable to escape, it became a real torment. Being pursued by a bible-thumping maniac is no joke and I was helpless to change things.

Another thing which was to make my life more miserable was the acquisition of a wind-up gramophone by my neighbour, the cook. Not only did he buy the infernal thing, but worst of all, he bought one record to go with it. One record of which only one side was ever used - the Andrew Sisters' rendering of "Singing Rum & Coca Cola". This was played over, and over, and over again. The thin partition bulkhead between my room and that of the cook did little to dampen the scratchy rendition of this piece of musical extravagance. Trying to study next door, I was literally driven up the wall. Rum and coca-cola does not mix at all well with algebra and physics, and much less, learning by heart the 31 articles of the Regulations for Preventing Collision at Sea (not that I had much time for that either).

Apart from a couple of excursions with the ship's agent to beaches on the north coast of the island, where the sea broke in spectacular surf, I have no other particular memories. I ate my first avocado pear ashore with the agent in a small restaurant in Port of Spain and I remember that the "natives" were not too friendly towards us "colonialists"!

Barbados, the next port of discharge, was much better. The islanders were kind and discharge was affected to barges out in the anchorage of Bridgetown where the water was so clear that I could see our anchor lying on the bottom.

Went ashore one night with the Second and the Fourth Engineers. Their interests were not so much in the local architecture and fauna, as in the varieties of rum available in the waterside bars. What one might call indigenous culture. Drinking only the famous coca-cola, I probably did not have the same perspective as my two friends who were obviously appreciating the different rums. Time passed, and one thing led to another.

They decided that it was time to sample the local girls who were even more plentiful than the varieties of rum. With a certain amount of delicacy, they felt that to lead me astray at my tender age might sit on their consciences, particularly if the "Old Man" got to hear of it. Nevertheless we had to stick together. There was nothing for it, therefore, but to drag me along with them to the local brothel indicated by the girls as being their place.

The engineers felt that their honour would be safe if they could save mine. They struck upon the idea that to do this, it was best that I should be tied up whilst they went about their business. Although I fought bravely, with the help of several of the girls who thought this extremely amusing, they lashed me to the banisters of the stairs leading to the rooms upstairs; these were painted bright green I remember. By this time though, I had lost whatever sense of humour I may have had at the beginning of this trying escapade.

I felt humiliated. We returned to the dock somewhat subdued to look for a boat to take us back to the ship. Having woken up a boatman we shakily climbed into a small leaking rowing- boat and started our half -mile journey back to the ship.

The night was hot and calm and the sea clearly reflected the stars. With the sound of the oars splashing quietly in the water we floated in darkness. I was shaken out of a hypnotic silence by the second engineer who, without any preamble, declared that if Jesus could walk on the water, then so could he. Whereupon he stood up and stepped off over the side onto the water. I say onto because from where I sat, I swear he took one step forward like in some film cartoon before disappearing beneath the surface. Fortunately he came back up quickly enough without my having to act the hero (by this time, the fourth was out for the count). Not being able to drag him back on board without capsizing the boat, I managed to hold him against the side and we trailed him back to the ship. By this time he had passed out. Getting him up the gangway was no mean task but at least the Barbadian boatman gave us a hand. He told me he knew all about Jesus walking on water.

Chapter 28

On completion of discharge we were told that we were to proceed in ballast to the island of Great Inagua which lies in the Bahamas, not far from the eastern tip of Cuba. There, we were to load a full cargo of salt in bulk.

For me, the passage to the Bahamas was spent in the holds, cleaning up after the last cargo and then whitewashing the bulkheads and decks with lime. Rigging stages to do this as the ship rolled and wallowed in the sea way was dangerous and tricky to say the least. Furthermore it was horrendously hot. The crew received extra pay for this. My participation in all this was conveniently forgotten.

Inagua was nothing more than a mosquito infested swamp with a vast salt lake at one end. There was absolutely nothing there but a few wooden tumbled-down shacks and buildings, and clouds of mosquitoes. The glare under the sun from the salt dumps was blinding.

As we started to load by means of grabs, William told me that I was to join a few of the seamen in the holds to assist them in trimming, or flattening out the pyramids of salt which accumulated in each hold as it was loaded. I was given a shovel and ordered to get on with it.

The only good thing about this was that there appeared to be fewer mosquitoes down below than on deck.

If there is a hell, it is certainly not composed of fire and brimstone. It is salt in the holds of an old tramp ship in temperatures approaching 40°C.

As the grabs were opened they released a mass of salt accompanied by clouds of fine salt-dust which found its way into ears, mouth, throat, eyes, and in fact, everywhere. This, mixed with perspiration, produced a burning brine solution. We had no form of protective clothing or goggles and worked barefoot, clothed only in shorts.

After the second day, I was covered from head to feet in a blistering skin rash. On the third day it turned into a bloody skin rash. Hell on earth. I now had a good idea of what a gulag salt- mine could be like. At the end of that day's work Mickey opened up a tin of butter which he applied and bandaged to the running sores and mosquito bites. This gave me some small relief. Since I was not the only one to suffer (we were all in the same condition), William decided that perhaps it was not really necessary, after all, to trim the rest of the salt which was to complete our cargo. In short, all this work for nothing.

It was a relief to leave this mosquito- infested island. Our destination was Kingston, Jamaica, a short run through the Windward Passage that separates Cuba from Haiti. We stayed there just long enough to discharge before proceeding in ballast to Georgetown, (British) Guyana. There, we loaded a full cargo of Demerara sugar in bags destined for Liverpool. By the time we had reached Georgetown, my salt burns had more or less healed and I was back on deck in the chipping rust business and trying to keep out of the way of my evangelical maniac. There was no escape however from the Andrew Sisters singing next door.

The only memory of Georgetown I have was an invitation to a reception at the British High Commissioner's residence. Afterwards, in the beautifully kept tropical gardens, the staff showed a film. It was an opportunity to wear my new starched white tropical uniform which I'd had made in Calcutta at a very reasonable price!

We arrived back in Liverpool, in December 1952. From the tropical gardens of the British High Commission to the docks in Liverpool was a shock. Nothing, however in comparison to what was about to happen.

During the discharge of the sugar I was given a couple of days leave only. Not much time for relaxation after a three months voyage. We were off again, this time in ballast to Narvik, Norway.

Christmas day was spent at sea in appalling weather conditions. With the ship in light condition, rolling on her beamends and being pitched up and down with the speed of a runaway express train, it was impossible to serve up proper meals so we went without. Back to the corned -beef again!

Narvik lies some two hundred and fifty miles north of the Arctic Circle on the north western coast of Norway. Not the ideal place to visit in January. In the first place, it is permanently night and secondly, navigation in the Arctic Ocean was, in those days, a bit of a hit and miss affair. Fortunately, not a lot of shipping about but at least the risk of icebergs is minimised by the effect of the Gulf Stream. It was, of course, bitterly cold and as we approached the coast of Norway, the seas and spray washing over the deck began to freeze in contact with the steelwork. The accumulated weight of ice on deck caused us to roll dangerously.

I must say that my greatcoat came in pretty useful for watch keeping after having been consigned to the back of my wardrobe. The problem was that it was not made for working on deck and working on deck became an essential part of survival as we reached the Lofoten Islands and headed up the Vestfjorden channel. The build-up of ice had reached proportions where the ship began to list heavily to starboard. Armed with crowbars, hammers and pieces of scrap metal from the engine-room, everyone who could be spared was turned out to break up the ice to try to shovel it overboard. Since we had no such thing as protective clothing or gloves, this operation in Arctic storm conditions in the dark, with icy spray blowing across the deck and freezing on one's oil skins, left a lot to be desired (I had occasion then, to bless Gardiners Naval Outfitters' salesman who had persuaded my mother that a hand -knitted woollen balaclava helmet was a necessary part of equipment for the well-being of the British seaman).

Snow covered Narvik, in the dark was not an attractive place, particularly alongside the iron ore berth allocated to us.

We were to load a cargo of iron-ore in bulk for discharge in Middlesbrough. The local method of doing this was simple. The berth had been cut out of the mountain side. High above the ship ran an embankment along which a railway line had been built. Wagons loaded with ore were shunted in line with the openings of the ship's holds and tipped over so that the contents would spill into a shute leading down the hillside and into the holds. This, in theory, was quite a good idea except for the fact that the iron ore took the form of rocks and stones and when tipped out from a great height, arrived into the hold in the form of an avalanche. The noise of rocks and boulders hitting the bottom and sides of the holds defies description. How the ore did not go right through the ship's sides I'll never know. Since night and day were for all intents and purposes the same, work was carried out twenty-four hours around the clock. Sleep was out of the question. Some of the ore in the wagons had frozen into a solid mass and required hammering, to break it out. For all that, it did not take too long before we were fully loaded, heading back out into the Arctic. Our destination was Middlesbrough.

It took only a few days to discharge in Middlesbrough and off we were again, back to Narvik for another load. Whilst I was in Middlesbrough I had managed to get ashore and bought another thick submariner sweater, gloves and socks. This, together with a long woollen scarf wound around my head, helped me to fight the cold, the snow and the ice.

The conditions were identical to those of the previous trip aggravated by the fact that we lost our port-side anchor in Narvik. Amidst the din, clatter and havoc of rocks and boulders rolling down the mountain side into the holds, on the ice covered deck, we struggled the shackle the spare anchor on to what remained of the cable. Not an easy job in the dark when the spare anchor is frozen into the fo'clehead bulkhead with rust and ice, particularly when the odd small boulder or rock would fly up out of the hold to fall back onto the deck, likely at any moment to decapitate you.

Back again to Middlesbrough to discharge. This time fortunately there was no call for us to return to Narvik. Instead, we loaded a general cargo and steel for the Persian Gulf. It was now the beginning of February 1953 and I had reached the age of nineteen.

Chapter 29

The voyage started well enough with a new crew and officers. The "Old Man", William, Chief and Second stewards together with the cook plus Andrew Sisters were still there of course, but at least the new Radio officer had little interest in the bible.

On arrival at Port Said prior to transiting the Suez Canal, I received a radio message from my father's friend, Richardson, who was then the managing director of a British shipping agency in Egypt He asked me to visit him on arrival at Port Said. He would arrange to send a boat for me whilst the ship was waiting its turn to enter the Canal, a matter of some six hours. At the same time Richardson sent a message to the "Old Man" asking if he would be kind enough to release me for the passage through the Canal in order that I should see something of the pyramids. He proposed that I should rejoin the ship at Suez as it left the Canal. The "Old Man's" reaction to this was that I was not on a holiday cruise. However I could visit Port Said for a couple of hours. No question of my visiting the pyramids.

It was with some surprise that once moored at the buoys in Port Said, the "Old Man", William and the cook, who had nothing better to do at that time, saw me in my best uniform, going down the gangway to board what could only be described as an Admiral's Barge, complete with sailors and petty officer in uniform.

I must admit that the reception I received was equal to that of a visiting V.I.P. Even captains do not have admiral's barges at their disposition. I was enormously flattered and extremely gratified that both the "Old Man" and William had witnessed this. A far cry from my reception on board the *Sunbridge* for the first time in Newport that grey, rainy day, two and a half years past.

The Richardsons treated me to cocktails and a magnificent dinner. I was extremely touched by their kindness and obvious fondness for my parents and sister. I was returned to the ship, late, just as she was sailing, with the same pomp and circumstance. My reception back on board was frigid. Being late, I was again reminded that I was not on a cruise.

On leaving the Red Sea, where the temperatures had crawled up into thirties with a following wind which meant that there was absolutely no breeze whatsoever, we called at Aden. There, we discharged a little of our cargo and bunkered before proceeding to Sharjah, Abu Dhabi and numerous small anchorage ports on the coast of Iran.

At anchor, off the small town of Bushihr, Iran, the heat was such that instead of working on deck during the afternoons I was allowed to work in the mornings, but only if I started at the crack of dawn. I started work therefore in the morning as soon as it became sufficiently light, thus avoiding a nasty dose of sunstroke. My task there was to repaint the plimsoll and load-line mark, overside on the hull plating in way of number 3 hatchway. A nice quiet job. I had rigged my stage and rope-ladder overside and was comfortably installed and busy with my paint and brushes. The sun had just risen, a red orb sitting on the horizon, and although it was hot, the temperature was bearable and as cool as it was likely to get. I sat, with my feet dangling in space, almost touching the surface of the sea which was as calm as a mill pond. All was silence and I was at peace with the world.

My reverie was disturbed by the sound of someone dragging something heavy and metallic along the deck above my head. I took no notice thinking that some of the crew had turned-to early like me to avoid the furnace heat of the afternoon.

Big, big mistake.

The noise stopped just overhead and mystified, I heard somebody struggling as though they were lifting a heavy weight. I was not mistaken. I looked up just as the mouth of the forty-gallon drum of galley garbage appeared over the gunwale. Too late to avoid it, I received the contents of days of rotting stinking food scraps, bones and peelings, full in the face.

Covered from head to foot in muck, I shot up my rope ladder and enraged, threw myself at the cook who had organised this little diversion with the help of one of the crew. Had I not been knocked senseless by hitting my head against the steel storm door at the entrance of the galley, I think I might have killed the cook. When I regained my senses I was lying on N.4 hatch, my head covered in a mixture of blood and garbage. The cook had disappeared into his room and barricaded the door.

Having finally completed discharge at Kuwait, we proceeded to Khorramshahr, Iran, and finally to Basra, Iraq, to load a part cargo of cased dates and other dried fruit for London. The return journey was without incident. We passed through Port Said at night I was therefore unable to see the Richardsons. We arrived back in London in late June 1953.

I was given two weeks leave and went home to Wickford a little older and wiser perhaps than when I had left it previously.

I can't remember how my leave passed but other than for two or three trips to London where I took some of Maureen's friends, girls from the convent, to the cinema. I stayed at home and tried to catch up on my studies which, by force of things, had been seriously neglected.

Our next trip was to be a little different. We were to be chartered by a prestigious French company in Le Havre and were to load a general cargo in France. After having drydocked in London we sailed in ballast for Le Havre where we were inspected by the company's superintendent and found suitable to load. They had intended to repaint us in their own colours but, on reflection, found us too antiquated to bear their livery and they left us in our own rusty colours.

Of the crew for that voyage, we had again got together a South Wales "crowd". Apart from that, the officers, stewards and, unfortunately, cooks, remained the same. The one big difference was the radio officer, Colm who after the second day on board seriously fell out with the "Old Man" and William. In the first place he was Irish and secondly, he was not very much older than me. Thirdly, he was cultivated, well educated and brilliant.

He had previously been articled to a Chartered Accountant in Dublin before deciding he needed a little adventure in his life. He had abandoned accountancy, entered a naval college in Dublin to train as Radio officer (then the most rapid way of getting to sea as an officer) and had joined the Peninsular & Orient Line as junior radio on one of their large liners serving the Far East. Junior officers in that company were kept very much in their place and no mixing with passengers was tolerated. Not much adventure for Colm who had dreamt of other things. He quickly left his white painted passenger ship and joined a British north east coast collier, all black, this time. This proved to be a wretched experience, quite beyond his wildest imagination. The dirt, impossible weather, poor food and men of a different world. My Newport, Narvik and Calcutta experiences all rolled into one. He decided to return to accountancy but before doing so, wanted to make one more attempt in the search of adventure.

He arranged to join the *Sunbridge* as Chief and only Radio officer. After the first couple of days aboard he began to realise his mistake but it was now too late; we were on our way and there was no turning back.

Left strictly alone these first few days on board, he had time to look around and assess his fellow officers. What he saw hardly encouraged him but he had caught sight of me in my far from clean dungarees and boots engaged in my daily tasks on deck and keeping watch on the four to eight.

Very rarely did I have the time to take my meals in the saloon but that first Sunday at sea on our way out to start loading in Bordeaux, I decided that it might be a chance to meet our new Radio officer, since he sat at my table. There, Colm told me of the beginning of his differences with the "Old Man" and William. I sympathised and very quickly we became friends. The first and only real friend I had during those awful, long four years on board the *Sunbridge*. A friendship that was to last for many years.

In Bordeaux, we loaded huge quantities of wine, of course, and general merchandise for discharge in Madagascar. Having saved a little money, I treated my new found friend to dinner ashore one evening. We dined in an upstairs room of a restaurant in a narrow street in the old town to the cries of swallows in the warm evening calm - a setting which I have never forgotten. For Colm, it was the first time that he had tasted French cuisine and I can even remember what we ate: pigeons aux petits pois, perhaps not something I would choose now but Colm was impressed particularly since it was served without potatoes. A meal without spuds was quite something, as was a bottle of Bordeaux wine!

From Bordeaux, we sailed for Sete via Gibraltar.

It was in Sete that I had arranged to meet my parents who were spending a couple of weeks in the Grand Hotel before crossing the Mediterranean to visit some remote cousins of my mother who owned large estates in and around Sidi bel Abes, near Oran, Algeria.

We only had a couple of days in Sete to load further quantities of wine but I managed to get ashore with Colm whom I introduced to my parents. We spent an afternoon on the beach before being treated to dinner - another first time experience for Colm, stuffed mussels, a Setoise delicacy and ratatouille with grilled lamb chops ; again no potatoes !

I had asked the "Old Man" for permission to bring my parents on board but this had been refused on the grounds that it was too dangerous whilst cargo was being loaded. I didn't press the matter too much, even though in Queensland, Australia, we had had many visitors, not forgetting the "nurses", during loading operations. Also, I was a little bit worried by my conditions on board and particularly of being next door to the cook, never quite knowing what he might get up to. A "Singing Rum and Coca-Cola" serenade at full blast, for example.

From Sete we crossed the Mediterranean bound for Algeria where we called at Mostaganem, near Oran to load more wine. At Mostaganem, I was taken ashore by the ship's forwarding agent from Oran who just happened to be another of my mother's distant cousins. Another part day-off; this was getting to be too much of a habit, the "Old Man" complained.

I am grateful for my visit to Oran and Mostaganem. I saw both of these beautiful towns, rich and prosperous. Sadly these conditions would soon end in war, destruction and bloodshed. From Mostaganem, we sailed for Algiers and Djibouti.

In Djibouti we discharged some of the wine and general cargo. I recall a party one night ashore in the company of Colm with some French Foreign Legionnaires. A massive booze-up! Our voyage continued to Madagascar.

The interminable trip to Tamatave was marked by a serious deterioration in the quality of our food. One evening, shortly before our arrival in Tamatave, I had just finished my meal in the officers' pantry as usual when I saw one of the able-seamen approaching with the crew "tea" in aluminium kits, one stacked upon the other. He was certainly excited about something and demanded to see the chief steward. As I watched, the altercation between the chief steward and the able-seaman escalated and ended with the seaman emptying the contents of the kits over the head of the chief steward. This comprised a watery, brown stew with bits of potatoes and cabbage. The same which I had just tried to eat a few moments earlier.

Lumps of fatty beef with gravy, slowly sliding down the chief stewards glasses was a sight for sore eyes. I think that when the able seaman thrust the container of stew under the chief steward's nose and demanded: "What the effing hell do you call this?", the chief steward should not, perhaps have said: "What's wrong with it?"

Unfortunately the able seaman in question, with whom I sympathised, was fined a couple of day's pay for this outrage. It did anything to improve the quality of the meals however.

It turned out that Colm was an enthusiastic small-boat sailor and had crewed regularly aboard a class of boats called Dublin Bay 24s. On arrival at Tamatave he was not slow in introducing himself to the local yacht club. Thereafter we both spent our evenings off work at the club where meals were available for visitors at very reasonable prices. Never did an omelette with a bottle of red wine taste so good.

Tamatave was a beautiful, gracious town in those days, with magnificent villas surrounded by well tended gardens, lawns and flowers in profusion; a little paradise on earth. From there, we headed up the east coast of Madagascar to Diego Suarez where we completed discharge. Diego Suarez was then a very substantial French naval base. Its natural harbour, one of the largest in the world, provided an ideal shelter for the biggest of warships and aircraft carriers.

Not very large, the town boasted of hundreds of girls, bars, cafés and restaurants. Colm and I arranged to get ourselves accepted into the Naval officer's Club, a beautiful colonial building with swimming pool surrounded by lawns and gardens where we spent as much time as we could to escape from the *Sunbridge* (Some years later, I was to return to Diego Suarez in very different circumstances. The clubhouse building was totally wrecked, derelict, its roof having fallen in. From the bottom of the pool a few miserable stunted trees and shrubs grew out of accumulated garbage and plastic bags. Everything had vanished, ships, girls, bars, restaurants, leaving nothing but a dusty rat infested tumble down ghost town).

Having completed discharge of our cargo which included large quantities of wines and other French delicacies, we left Madagascar in ballast for Port Louis, Mauritius, where we were to load a cargo of raw sugar for Tacoma, West coast of the USA.

Although I had little time to visit the island, I was able to see some of its magnificent beaches, then totally unspoilt by the construction of tourist hotels. This was thanks to the ship's agent's family who very kindly took me under their wing each evening during our short stay.

Loading completed, we headed out across the Indian Ocean, to Singapore and Honolulu and across the North Pacific Ocean to Tacoma, more than half way around the world.

An interminable trip during which I was told that I was to strip and re-varnish all the bridge accommodation woodwork. This comprised tongue and groove mahogany planking which ran across the bridge front and around the upper and lower bridge wings ; a monumental task. Varnishing was one thing, but stripping years of layers of old cracked and peeling varnish was altogether another. No such thing as paint remover or sanding machine. Just a concentrated solution of caustic soda and hard work with a triangular scraper.

Blisters and caustic soda burns on face and hands became the order of the day. Resorted again to the butter bandage treatment. Week after week it lasted mostly under a blazing sun, suspended in the air above the hatchway of N.2 hold, swaying backwards and forwards as the ship rolled and pitched. I scraped and scraped (my father used to say that if a job was worth doing, it was worth doing well). By the time we reached the west coast of the USA, the bridge superstructure of the *Sunbridge* gleamed like new in the sun for all to see. It had nearly crippled me but it was all my own work and had it been my own yacht I could not have been more pleased with the results.

Our cargo of sugar was rapidly discharged and for once it was not necessary for me to help in washing out the holds. It was obligatory to use shore labour for this.

I have one vivid memory of Tacoma. Literally hundreds of wartime Liberty ships and destroyers all lined up, row upon row, "Mothballed", it was said. Were the Americans waiting for another big war to bring them all out into service once more, I wondered.

From Tacoma we worked our way into the creeks of Puget Sound and Vancouver Island to load sawn timber at various points wherever sawmills were located. Access to these places seemed to be for the most part by seaplane. Just hundreds of miles of magnificent conifer forest and little else. Beautiful, clean, virgin country, totally unspoilt. Having completed loading, piled high with timber on deck, we sailed for Liverpool via the Panama Canal.

We finally arrived in Liverpool just before Christmas 1953. A couple of days to discharge the deck cargo and we were back at sea on our way to Barry Dock, South Wales where we arrived and berthed on Christmas Eve.

Chapter 30

Christmas at home! Two weeks leave; things were looking up. Somewhat isolated in Innes House, I took advantage of the fact by trying to catch up on my studies. We were now in 1954, the year in which I would have to decide what to do with my life. But before then, almost another year to survive onboard the *Sunbridge*! The two weeks at home which I had been accorded passed too quickly and it was back to Barry docks.

For the coming voyage we had been chartered by Port Line, a prestigious company serving Australia and New Zealand with cargo-passenger liners. It seemed that the old *Sunbridge* was to receive a face-lift in the form of a total repaint job in Port Line colours. In my best uniform, I was to accompany William, the Port Line superintendent and a company director in their inspection of the *Sunbridge* which, the day previously, had been swept, by me of course, as clean as it was possible. The pile of galley garbage had been hidden beneath a nice new hatch tarpaulin (to be quickly recovered before it could be stolen as soon as the inspection had passed). We could not do much about the hull, which was rust streaked and black whereas that of Port Line ships was an impeccable dove -grey. The Port Line funnel, their pride and joy, was similar to that of Cunard; imagine the prestige! Ours, which it had been my privilege to repaint several times at the cost of burnt knees and elbows, in the last few years, had faded from bright red to a dull, rust streaked, faded pink.

I could tell, from the way their superintendent minced around the deck, that he did not think much of our potential and that his sole preoccupation was to get down the gangway as quickly as possible and get back to London.

The idea of giving the old girl a face-lift was abandoned needless to say. We were not even to fly their house flag colours from our mainmast. I was mortified - after all the sweeping up and vanishing I had done.

Notwithstanding all this, we were, in fact, to carry general cargo to Adelaide and Melbourne, even if it meant sneaking around the coast incognito. The day before sailing, on my twentieth birthday, William instructed me to open up the old cross-bunker and get it ready to load straw, hay and fodder. I was to resume my role as stable -lad (unpaid). We were to load two race horses for Adelaide. Two is exactly twice as much work as one , my poor maths told me, and added to this was the fact that a trip to Australia takes three times the time it took to cross the Atlantic. This did not speak well for my future study periods.

The crew we embarked was from South Wales as usual. By now I had achieved a certain status amongst the sailors. I could splice mooring wires, ropes, rig and un-rig derricks faster than any of them and even if I still polished the bridge brass-work, I was allowed to take compass bearings and sometimes, was entrusted with a sextant to take a "sight", which, so far as they were concerned, put me more or less onto a different social plane. Colm, out of friendship for me, decided to make another voyage on the *Sunbridge* which cheered me up immensely.

Apart for my friendship with Colm which counted for a lot towards my sanity, I can't recall much about the voyage to Australia. I took on all the work, and more, that was thrown at me and bore all the scorn with equanimity that the "Old Man" and William still used on me.

Although far from being "keen" on animals, I struck up a close companionship with my two horses, particularly one week or so after having sailed from London, in the Eastern Mediterranean when we ran into a hurricane force storm ; the worst seas in fact that I had ever seen or was ever to see.

Both horses had been ill from the moment we had left the English Channel. After passing Gibraltar, they settled down a bit and we got to know each other and just as they were beginning to perk up, we were laid flat on our beam - ends for two days and nights just before arriving at Port Said. With seas washing down the deck and heavy spray beating against the horse-boxes, I stayed up with the horses throughout, doing my best to calm and soothe them. They were in such a state that I thought I might loose them both.

Somehow, they recovered and I considered myself as some super veterinary officer, proud of my stable- side manner.

On passing through the Suez Canal, in the same convoy, I saw the French transatlantic liner "Pasteur", easily identifiable by its huge funnel, loaded to overflowing with French troops, boys of my age, on their way to Indochina (many of them were to be massacred some time later by the Vietminh at Dien Bien Phu). As I saw them, cheerfully ignorant of what was to befall them, I told myself that I had no real cause to complain when the cook emptied the galley gash over my face.

After Suez came the tropics, the heat, and by the time the horses arrived in Adelaide, regardless of my having fed, cleaned and looked after them as best I could, they looked ready for the knackers' yard. It seemed, however, that my services had been appreciated after all for I received the princely sum of five pounds from William. This act of generosity led me to believe that another large brown envelope had been passed to him under the table. Still, this was definitely a step in the right direction.

Australia, and the rest of the world, was changing. The Australians no longer needed us as they had in 1950. They were expanding rapidly, manufacturing their own goods and tramp ships were becoming superfluous to the liner companies. We were not able to find a cargo from Australia and were forced to return to England via the Cape of Good Hope in ballast. We arrived, in Liverpool, during the middle of June 1954.

Home for a few days only, then back to the *Sunbridge.*

This time, we were chartered by Palm Line for one round voyage, there and back to West Africa. This news should have cheered our Nigerian cooks but in fact, they appeared instead to be somewhat apprehensive about the prospects of returning to their own part of the world. Perhaps they already had some idea of what was coming.

During the last couple of voyages, Colm had described his sporting activities aboard fantastic gaff rigged racing yachts, the Dublin Bay 24s. Whilst I had always been interested in sailing, these stories fired my imagination and I decided that having a few days leave in Wickford, I would go to Burnham-on-Crouch, only a few miles away, and see for myself what the world of yachting might offer.

Next to the Cowes, Burnham was probably one of the most important centres of yachting in England. The most eye catching building on the water-front of Burnham was, and still is, the clubhouse of the Royal Corinthian Yacht Club. Impressed, I looked around and told myself that here was something more in my line. I now had a goal, something to aim for. A boat of my own and membership of the Royal

Corinthian Yacht Club. I could hardly get back fast enough to Liverpool to tell Colm of my discovery.

Colm, in the meantime had returned home to Dublin. Initially, he had decided that he was not returning to the *Sunbridge*, but changed his mind at the last moment. I think that the decision to make this one last voyage, on the *Sgeunbrid* was to have a radical effect on his life. During the last voyage to Australia he had developed a short, nasty nervous dry cough. The voyage we were about to undertake would do nothing to improve his situation. Nevertheless, for a trip to West Africa, "White Man's grave" and all that, he came prepared. Cough mixtures of various colours, kaolin plaster, the works, leaving nothing to chance.

Chapter 31

We left England in June 1954, loaded with all manner of general cargo, including several hundred tons of Heineken beer which subsequently was to cause us a lot of trouble. The deck was cluttered up with heavy machinery, trucks and mining equipment.

Our first port was Freetown, not a place where one might wish to spend a holiday. It was my first encounter with Africa in the raw and I did not think that it had changed much since the first missionaries had set foot in Sierra Leone; open drains and rusty corrugated iron.

Our deck cargo was discharged and in its place we embarked about a hundred Africans who were to live on deck and provide the labour to discharge, and subsequently load cargo for the duration of the voyage until our return to Freetown, homeward bound, some three months later.

The crushing humidity, the heat, flies, mosquitoes, cockroaches and the smell, overpowered us. We had been turned into a sort of floating, tropical gulag.

The Africans, or crew boys as they were called, split into teams, each with its headman who enforced law and order, of sorts, with a club or pickaxe handle (we had lots of the latter amongst the cargo), and a cook. Two cast-iron, steam rice-boilers, looking very much like the same pots that were used by the natives to cook missionaries, were welded onto the deck in the lee of the fo'cle and poop and connected up to the deck steam line serving the cargo winches. This had a particular inconvenience for me since the deck steam-line ran the length of the alleyway just outside my cabin.

Although lagged with asbestos, the heat in my cabin generated by this was appalling.

Fresh water was supplied by the ship by way of the galley hand-pump, located just outside my alleyway door; a continual clanking of the iron pump handle. The commotion caused by this, night and day, drove me mad.

Hygiene was simple; it took the form of standing in the way of the salt-water fire hydrants on deck. In guise of latrines, paint stages were rigged overside, around the stern of the ship. Nothing could be more simple, providing you did not fall off the stage into the crocodile infested waters below.

I didn't look too closely, but their food comprised boiled rice, mixed with black things which may have been beans or cockroaches mixed with fish which they caught themselves: horrible evil-looking cat- fish.

For myself, in port, I was condemned with the rest of the seamen to working all hours amidst this multitude, repairing broken rigging cargo gear, wires, ropes and hatch- boards.

Having embarked the "crew boys", we sailed around the coast to Lagos to commence discharge of the under-deck general cargo, a trip of about five days. Torn pieces of old tarpaulin, flour sacks and gunny bags lashed together with bits of string and broken planks flourished on deck in the form of shelters. We looked like a cross between a floating shanty -town and an embarkation of poor Vietnamese boat people darkened by the sun.

Lagos was hardly a tourist attraction and I remember little of that first visit except that it comprised buildings with painted corrugated iron roofs, giving even the government establishments a temporary look. From there, we headed up the creeks, literally, of the mouths of the river Niger, to

Sapele and to Warri, small depressing fever ridden towns. Mosquitoes, humidity and equatorial forest.

I recall that to find ones way up these rivers we required the services of a pilot. The pilots were local Africans who, like pirates, lay in wait for ships to arrive. Once sighted, they would paddle out in their dugout canoes, sometimes three or four at a time and race out to try and board by way of a rope ladder thrown over the side. First one there got the job. It was not unusual for two pilots to arrive alongside at the end of the ladder at the same time. A punch-up followed as the ship steamed onward without slackening speed, to the merriment of the "Old Man" who considered this an entertaining sport. Pilots were paid in cash according to how they performed.

Running aground into a mud bank and having to haul oneself off by mooring lines attached to trees was not unusual. At night it was customary to anchor to await daybreak, there being no navigational lights or buoys to show the way. Since the creeks were narrow, winding and shallow, the blind bends were numerous. The tricky part was approaching one of these without being able to see what was coming round the bend. No VHF in those days! I suppose that it didn't happen often, but it happened to us. Rounding a bend on the way out of Sapele, we found ourselves face to face with a heavily loaded Palm Line ship somewhat larger than us. There was just enough room for us to pass but not without one of us giving way and running aground. Needless to say, we saw no reason why it should be us who should run ourselves into the mud. We both crashed together, our anchor got itself all mixed up with the rails of their fo'clehead and we both ended up stuck in the mud, having demolished part of the river bank and brought down several trees; this delighted our crew boys.

It took us a couple of days to extricate ourselves during which I had time to exchange notes with the Cadet Officers (all in pristine whites), of the other ship; another world. They actually received proper lessons each day in navigation, maths and the like. They did not mix with the crew, nor were they sent aloft to paint the funnel or, for that matter, overside, on stages, to paint the ship's side.

We duly arrived at Port Harcourt, the last Nigerian town of any size before the Cameroon border. Here, the "Old Man" ran into big trouble, as did the rest of the officers and the deck crew. During the voyage, the crew, who had got to know the layout of the stowage of cargo in the holds, had burrowed their way down through a mass of cases of general goods to the stowage of hundreds of cartons of Heineken beer. No wonder they had all been so cheerful throughout the run from Freetown.

When we came to discharge the beer at Port Harcourt, it was discovered that a very substantial part of the consignment was missing. The cartons were still there of course, but the contents had disappeared; hundreds of bottles, without a trace.

The "Old Man" was arrested by the police and taken ashore where, no doubt, the matter was amicably settled for he came back to the ship with the air of a man well pleased with himself. I think that Colm and I must have been about the only ones aboard who had not been aware of the beer finding its way out of the hold.

Colm, by this time, was not well. He was coughing a lot and spent his days hidden away in the wireless-room in a private world of his own. He had again fallen out seriously with both the "Old Man" and William.

Our food was another thing: no potatoes, only yams. Poor Colm could not stomach yams and he began to lose weight.

At Port Harcourt we turned around for the homeward voyage and started loading logs. We called at a place called Bonny which was a misnomer if there ever was one, and then on to Takoradi, Gold Coast (now Ghana) to load cocoa.

Takoradi was the scene of my last serious brush with the crew who after the beer, were hung over and had lost their bonhomie. Ordered overside to paint the ship's side, they were disgruntled and slow particularly when it came to working aft where the crew-boys did their daily business. For the duration of the painting operation, their stages, fortunately, had been moved forward but it was still what one might call a danger zone.

It was now getting near the end of my "time" and I would soon be leaving the ship for good. It was time, then, for one last, good lesson of humility. I was ordered by William to repaint the stern. Knowing that I had been manipulated by the crew, I sought refuge in a certain arrogance. I started complaining to my "handlers" that my stage ropes were improperly secured, were too tight, were not in the right place, all of which, I may say, was more or less true.

When at last I was dangling over the side and finally settled with my pot of black paint, long handled scraper and brush, I had the feeling that something was wrong. The rope at one end of my stage had not been correctly tied and started slipping. The pot of paint tipped over me as I made a grab for the rope ladder leading back up to the deck. I missed it as one side of the stage suddenly fell away leaving it virtually suspended by one end. From a great height, covered in black paint, I fell into the sea.

Now, a nice blue sea is one thing, but the open sewer that served Takoradi harbour, was another. I felt that I had swallowed half of that sewer before I manage to heave myself out onto rat infested pilings beneath the quayside. I was finally rescued by an African in a dug-out canoe and duly returned on board, sick and wondering if I would survive. Strangely enough, I did, without any after-effects.

Perhaps this was thanks to the Chinese anti-plague vaccination.

I refused to return to my painting and took a day off. I think that perhaps William may have thought that he had gone a bit too far in "shaping" me up, for after that incident, he left me alone, not exactly kind to me, but very wary of upsetting me again.

We completed loading and made our way up to Freetown to disembark our crew-boys.

What a relief it was to be able to clean up, open the accommodation and head out into the Atlantic Ocean. We were still eating yams of course, but at least we were heading north.

We rounded the North West cape of Spain and entered the Bay of Biscay on the 20th October 1954, exactly four years after having stepped aboard the *Sunbridge* in Newport. Nothing very much had changed since that time. I was still on the four to eight watch with William, spent my days in dungarees which by now had acquired a decidedly tatty look, and took most of my meals, for what they were worth, in the officer's pantry with Mickey.

Mickey, during the past four years, had been a friend and had supplied me with quantities of hot buttered toast at six o'clock in the mornings when I came off the wheel. Normally this was the best part of the day, especially when I'd had my horses. In fine weather, sitting on the tarpaulin cover of number 3 hatchway outside the pantry, eating my toast and drinking coffee was about as close to heaven as I could get.

On the subject of the anniversary, I thought it best not to remind anyone, not knowing quite how such news might be greeted. I did, though, confide in Colm. We had nothing with which to celebrate, for other than the weekly rum-ration dished out to the crew each Saturday before "tea", no alcohol was allowed on board - officially that is.

In the Bay of Biscay we were swept by a severe storm. Back to biscuits and corned-beef. Our destination was Hamburg, followed by Rotterdam where the voyage was to terminate.

Hamburg, I found to be a dreary, wet, cold city, very knocked about during the war and under full reconstruction. Shortage of everything and an active black market (Hamburg was to be, a few years later, the scene of my last serious punch-up; a round of fisticuffs with a woman of easy virtue which I lost. She didn't play fairly, but that's another story).

Whilst almost the totality of the officers and crew disappeared ashore in the direction of the Reeperbahn, where the night life and girls of the city were concentrated, I remained on board having been appointed night watchman.

Now I felt that I had really sampled all possible professions!

On completion of discharge, we shifted to Rotterdam where I learnt that my home for the last four years had been sold as scrap-iron and was to be broken up.

It cannot be said that during this time I had been particularly happy, but the knowledge of the old *Sunbridge* being cut up into pieces, stirred within me a profound sense of regret. Perhaps a touch of the Stockholm syndrome. Had I not chipped and scraped, painted, to say nothing of vanishing the old girl, to keep her looking young and sprightly?

On the day I paid-off, the "Old Man" sent for me and told me that my examination results of the past had not been brilliant and that I had best knuckle down to my studies to pass my Second Mate's Certificate. I shall never ever forget the sense of outrage that filled me at that time. I hardly expected any thanks for all my efforts but received nothing, not a word of encouragement, nothing.

My other farewells were brief but generally warm and even William appeared to be sincerely sorry to see me go. I had the feeling that his own sailing days were over and for the first time in four years, I saw him unsure of himself, quite overtaken by the events. I even felt a little sorry for him. It was probably the same for the Chief Engineer who would return to his Yorkshire strong ales, but who would have considerable trouble. I think, in finding another berth. The same would apply to the Second and Third Engineers and Chief steward, all worn-out survivors of the war for whom the Sunbridge had been a haven and refuge from a rapidly changing modern world that now had no place for such men. Out of them all, only the "Old Man" and Mickey would survive.

Colm and I left the ship together as she was being divested of the last drums of paint, ropes, wires and other removable objects, including the spare anchor, on the morning of the 3rd November 1954, four years and fourteen days after "Newport".

It was a bright, blustery day and the crossing from the Hook of Holland to Harwich blew away the sense of anticlimax that had settled over me. I was free. I had fulfilled my contract with both my father and the company. It was time to turn the page.

Colm, who had become a close friend, told me that he intended to give up the sea. In fact, after his return home, it was diagnosed that he suffered from advanced tuberculosis. He spent a full year on his back in an Irish sanatorium and duly recovered. During that time, he studied marine biology, obtained his degrees and eventually a doctorate.

Chapter 32

I must admit returning home to Wickford with a certain sense of achievement. I had done what I had set out to do. There had been no short cuts and it had been hard, even by the standards of the period (I was to learn subsequently that in most shipping companies it was expressly forbidden for cadets to mix with the crew. They were not to be sent aloft to work on topmasts, nor were they allowed to paint overside on stages, nor in fact, were they forced to paint funnels from swinging bosun's chairs. All of this, and more, I had done without even thinking that others like me were protected by such things as company regulations, Factories Acts and the like).

There was one thing, though, that needed sorting out. I'd not had a lot of time to study and I knew from my last examinations results, that I had a lot of catching up to do before I could sit my Second Mate's certificate. I would have to go back to school. This didn't enchant me but if I was to profit from what I'd done, there was no alternative.

My enquiries into this led me to King Edward VII Nautical College in Limehouse, London, where preparatory courses for Second Mates were held. The college stood at the top end of West India Dock road opposite Gardiner's Naval Outfitters, a few doors away from the church of St Anne's, built in 1712, a haven of peace and quiet between the riverside wharves, brewery and the heavy traffic of Commercial road.

The college, being in London, was within daily reach of Wickford. Not easy, since I had to walk to Wickford, then train to Liverpool Street station, then walk to Aldgate, and finally, bus-ride down to Limehouse ; a door to door trip of about two and a half hours each way. Courses started at nine the morning and finished at four or four thirty in the afternoon, five days a week. This meant that I had to get up in the morning at around six o'clock. Not too hard, but awful when it was dark, cold and raining. Worse was the mud of the unlit, unmade road.

The course started in January 1955. I had a couple of months at home therefore to prepare, buy books and adapt to life ashore.

During these first two months ashore, not a lot happened. It was dark and wet, a far cry from the beaches of Honolulu. I saw a few plays in the West End and took out a couple of Maureen's friends, slightly boisterous girls from the convent : nothing serious and anyway the opportunities of meeting other girls during that period were few and very far between.

So started a period about which I have very few recollections. The daily grind of commuting to London and back. The bad weather, runny noses, packed trains and busses and hoards of people. The course was like being back at school, sport and gym being replaced by signals and the Uniform System of Maritime Buoyage. Again, as I look back, there didn't seem to be much time left for amusement. A quick pint in the pub on Friday lunchtimes after having collected the dole from the local unemployment exchange. Yes, I was now in the big money.

Although I was not what one might call a star pupil, I gradually made up for the "lost" time at sea and after several months I sat my Second Mates exam.

Whilst I passed all the written papers, I had some problem with the oral examination. It was my misfortune to have, as examiner, my old sparring partner, the man in charge of the red, green and white/yellow lantern slide show. He remembered me, or at least my name, even after four years. The first part of the examination passed without any significant problems and after about half an hour of hard questioning he told me to fetch a pair of wooden-handled semaphore signalling flags from a corner of the room. He told me exactly where to stand in the middle of the floor. This puzzled me; why so precise? I was instructed to send him back a series of coded messages as he called them out. Fine, I had no problem with that. Unfortunately, he had stood me directly beneath the central ceiling light fitting; a large white glass bowl that hung low. Concentrating on what I was being told to send, I flung up my arms holding the flags in the prescribed manner to commence sending back the message. There was a crash and a shower of broken glass. I had smashed the light-fitting. I'll not repeat what I was called. He almost literally threw me out of the room and told me not to come back for at least a month. I had failed my orals. It seemed that an officer incapable of being able to see the score and look around him could not be of much use when the chips were down.

When I returned one month later I had the good luck to be re-examined by another examiner with whom I had no problem. After only about fifteen minutes he let me go, telling me that I had passed.

I had my Second Mates certificate and it was time to see exactly what I wanted to do with it.

The pleasure this news gave to my parents was well worth all the effort and work that I had put in. Father visited a nautical instrument shop in the City and bought me a sextant. An exceptionally handsome one which I used throughout the whole of my career at sea. I have it still and treasure it to this day.

It's sad in a way, but it was to be very many years before I finally admitted to Father that my life aboard the *Sunbridge* had not been exactly a bed of roses. He was genuinely surprised and asked me why I had not told him so at the time; he said that he might have been able to do something to make my life easier. For me, however, at that time it was a matter of seeing just how far I could be pushed before I gave up.

Chapter 33

After the results of the examination had been published I had received offers of employment from a number of shipping companies. Cargo-liner companies, China coast, West Africa and Pacific Ocean routes. In addition, to my entire amazement, I received a letter from the "Old Man" of the *Sunbridge* who had been offered another command and wanted me to join him as his Third Officer. I thanked him and told him that I had not yet made up my mind with regard to the future.

That, in fact, was the truth. I'd had enough tramping around the world and was looking for something different. Amongst the offers I received was a letter from the Admiralty which at that time was keen on recruiting pilots for the Fleet Air Arm. I wrote back saying I was interested and in due course they sent me an application form. I completed this and returned it. I then had to wait for a date on which I was to go to Portsmouth for interviews, aptitude tests and medical examination.

In the meantime I began to think about what life might be like serving on a passenger liner.

My thoughts turned to the magnificent lavender-hulled ships I had seen in Cape Town and Southampton. In my travels I'd heard that such ships sailed only with officers who'd had considerable previous senior watch-keeping experience. Still, I thought, no harm in trying, particularly since I'd heard that the earliest date for interview for the Fleet Air Arm in Portsmouth was not be for another three months. So, I wrote to the Union-Castle Mail Steamship

Company in London and asked them, tongue in cheek, if there were any vacancies.

By return of post I was surprised to receive a friendly letter asking me to visit them at their head office in Fenchurch Street at my convenience. No sooner said than done, I put on my best suit and took the train to London.

I was most impressed by the size and opulence of their building and offices which were a far cry from those of Sundale in nearby St Helen's Place. I was greeted with warmth and courtesy, and rather than being interviewed, the marine superintendent ran me through a short history of the Union-Castle Line and explained the working of their different services and what would be required of me in general. Almost without realising it, I signed a two-year contract and became a part of the seagoing staff of what was then still almost a family company.

There are many stories which I might have called to mind and written here. Whilst some might have been more amusing or technically interesting than those I have already told, I feel that perhaps it's time to stop. I am sorry that I have written little about all those around me who throughout my early life, gave me love, courage and support. My parents, my sister and many friends scattered throughout the world whom I hold dear.

Printed in Great Britain
by Amazon